Enter the Abyss

A SHORT STORY COLLECTION

by

Eric Bonholtzer

A Division of Wise Bear, Inc.
Los Angeles, California

ENTER THE ABYSS

Printed in the United States of America

Published by Wise Bear Media
Los Angeles, California
www.wisebearmedia.com

Paperback ISBN: 978-1-939111-02-9
E-Book ISBN: 978-1-939111-03-6

Dedication

For my wife, Anastasia, my love always.

For my family:
Suzie, Craig, Trent, Taty, Joan, Jack, Gigi, George,
and all the friends too numerous to mention.
Your never-ending love and support
means the world to me.

Contents

A Grave Situation

Digging graves was not a desirable occupation. The dirt was unforgiving, cold and solid. It was back-breaking work, a bone-wearying profession. Max had known all of this before he had taken the job, but sometimes circumstances dictated the situation. He had a problem, and try as he might, his hands just always seemed to wander where they didn't belong and return with something that wasn't theirs.

But Max was an optimist. No matter how far he sank, he always considered it a temporary plight. He could dig graves. He could till the earth's surface for as long as it took because after all, it was still just a temp job. Now, almost six months after being released from the county lockup, Max began to wonder just how long this living hell was going to last. His Uncle John, the graveyard caretaker, a gruff old man with a toothless grin and a lazy eye, had told Max when he'd started off that he'd be digging graves until he dug his own, and at the time, Max could barely suppress a chuckle, but now he wasn't so sure.

As Max's dirt-encrusted pick split the grass, his thoughts wandered. He wondered how, for a town of only 500 people, they could manage a body or two a week. Sure, threshers hacked people to death. Farm animals killed ranchers in freak accidents. And there was a staggering cancer rate; these people smoked like the Marlboro man was riding away with the last of their cigarettes. But still, it just seemed like a bad town, a place where people came to die.

Max's current client, though, had been a transient. A bad car accident and no one to claim the remains. Not a particularly pleasant way to go. Max paused, lit up a cigarette, and thought that, perhaps, there weren't all that many ways that were. Inhaling deeply, Max listened to the faint rumblings of thunder just over the hills, telling of the storm to come.

He had to hurry. There was still another body waiting on the table, an old drunk named Howard Broach, who had to be interred before the storm made the ground too muddy to till. Max's thoughts grew grimmer contemplating that enormously corpulent deceased, whose only legacy in life was to indulge everything to excess and leave an immensely bloated corpse behind. And while there were no shortages of mourners at his funeral, when all the smoke settled, no one wanted to be stuck with the bill. Howard Broach became another county job. Max had been sour at the funeral and he was sour now. County requisitioned bodies, those with no one to claim them, were interred for next to nothing, which made Max's cut even less. With a grimace, he snuffed out his cigarette with a booted toe, took a swig of whiskey from the flask he always kept at the ready, and returned to his digging.

Night had fallen by the time the two holes were dug, and with great effort, Max wrested the bodies into their final homes, the unwieldy body of the late Howard Broach giving him more than a little trouble. Max had asked his uncle about a coffin for the body and the man had merely shrugged. The county got what it paid for.

With a grunt, Max picked up his shovel and somberly started filling in the graves. Rain was beginning to fall, making the grip more slippery with every stroke of the shovel. "Damn," Max groaned as the spade slid out of his hand, down onto the barely covered body of Howard Broach. Max shook his head in aggravation as he climbed down into the muddy hole, cursing his misfortune. As he bent down to retrieve the implement near a bloated hand that appeared to be reaching out of the dirt for a lifeline, suddenly, Max's run of bad luck seemed to come to a dead halt. Fortune surely smiled on him as his eye caught a glimmer that could only be gold, a ring still attached to the dead man's finger. It was a plain gold band with ruby inlay set in a distinct pattern. Definitely valuable. Perhaps tonight had not been such a bust after all.

Curious as to why his uncle, by no means an honest man, had not thought of the same idea, Max bitterly found out the reason as he tried to wrest the ring from the corpse. Stuck tight. Judging from the frayed and torn skin on the bloated finger, Max realized his uncle *had* come up with the same idea and had obviously failed. Not wanting to follow in his uncle's footsteps, Max simply seized the burial spade and hacked off the finger with a single stroke, easily extricating the ring. Prize in hand, Max climbed from the grave, tossing the finger over his shoulder with no more thought than a discarded cigarette butt.

After relishing his treasure for a few golden moments, a subtle fear began to gnaw at him, realizing what he had just done. Thoughts of cold clammy hands bursting from the grave flashed through Max's mind with every scoop of dirt as he quickly resumed his job of interment. Max could almost feel that cold lifeless stare watching him, waiting for something. "Sorry buddy, you're not getting your ring back," Max muttered under his breath. "Finders keepers. You're not going to need it where you're going." As sweat beaded his brow, Max swore, as he shoveled the last patches of dirt over Howard "Nine Fingers" Broach, that the corpse's eyes were wide open.

✷ ✷ ✷

Max's house was little more than a shanty, the paint peeling and the floorboards creaking, but the refrigerator was filled with cool beer and that was enough. A pile of discarded tall cans later and the grave digger was feeling A-OK. The TV, with its blurred picture, was off, but the radio bleated a bluesy tune and a new found sense of possibility flared in the soon-to-be-former grave digger.

Max pulled out the ring and fingered his prize gently, marveling at the uncanny smoothness. Despite the glow of intoxication slowly enveloping him, something didn't set right about it, and Max knew it wasn't pangs of regret. There was definitely something *off* about the ring, and its ruby inlay, but Max couldn't pinpoint it, and furthermore, he didn't really care. It was his ticket out. The money it would fetch at hock would set him up for a while until he could find something better. Tossing a discarded can to lay with the others, Max searched for another beer. Finding it, he popped the lid and spilled the drink all over himself as he heard a voice.

It was old and hollow, as if from a great distance away, calling out to him, *"My ring."* Max shivered, glancing around frantically. He was alone. Or so it seemed. He tried to tell himself it was just an overactive imagination and too many graveyard stories, but he wasn't convinced. Trying to salvage what was left of his beer, he came up with only two shallow sips. He *definitely* needed another one.

Max made his way to the kitchen, flicking on the light switch as he went. A little illumination and a fresh can of beer did wonders to ease the mind. He was already halfway to feeling normal again when he saw it. Muddy footprints. And definitely not his own. Following the dirty trail led a bewildered Max back into his living room.

Sitting there patiently was none other than Mr. Howard "I'm Buried" Broach, a sickly pallor coupled with dirt-stained clothes.

"What... what... the..." Max could barely voice the words, taking a tentative step back as he spoke them. "What... what... do you want?"

Howard chuckled, an animal-like cackle. *"What do I want? Hmmm... now let me see?"* As the unreality of it all set in, Max suppressed a scream. *"Well a coffin would have been nice."* Again that horrid laugh. *"Maybe someone who wouldn't have tossed me into the dirt. Yeah, you thought I didn't see, well I was watching. But you know what I really want? I want my finger back."* That same humorless smile never leaving his face, Howard held up his mangled hand short one digit.

Max took another step back, his mind unable to handle the unreality of it all. He searched frantically for a weapon but found nothing promising. *"Forget it. What's a little finger between friends, right? But you do have something I really want back, Maximillion. My ring. It's special. You like the ruby pattern? The ancient Byzantine symbol for immortality? I know I did. It called to me Max, like it called to you. I knew from the second I saw it on that gypsy's finger. I knew I'd kill for it. It speaks to you, Max. But you already knew that didn't you? I feel its voice waning in me, and I need it. It does things Max... It'll bring me back. Forever."*

Despite his fear, Max realized just how much his *own* future rested with that ring. It was his, and nobody was going to take that from him. If it truly was that powerful it would be priceless. Max stalled for time, "What ring?"

"MY RING!!! I want my ring now!"

Max took another backward step, running into a wall, his hands going up protectively. "It's my ring now."

His eyes closed despite himself and he waited for those cold hands that never came.

Instead there was just horrid laughter. *"Over your dead body, right?"*

After several moments passed and Max found himself still alive, he mustered the courage to open his eyes. Nothing. He was alone again. Utterly alone this time. He checked his pocket, the ring still nestled safely inside; his eyes catching on the pile of discarded beer cans. Had he really had that many? He didn't feel drunk, but he knew he probably was. He tried to rationalize. It had to have been a hallucination. Stress and alcohol were never a good mix. That was the only explanation. And nearly an hour later, after a few more tall ones, as Max slipped into sleep, he had a good long laugh about the whole thing.

* * *

Sleep didn't last long. The peal of the thunder awakened Max in a cold sweat. He was still in the throes of a waking dream, the vision earlier still all too real. For the next hour he tried to fall back asleep, but with little success. The storm had abated somewhat, but he couldn't shake what he had seen. Every time he shut his eyes he could see cold dead hands digging their way towards him. Another two hours of restless waking, debating on the reality of his encounter, and a full bottle of Jack Daniels later, Max reached a conclusion: he knew what he had to do.

The rain beat down on him like miniscule needles. Max would make sure it was just his mind playing tricks on him and then he would go home reassured. He was thoroughly soaked by the time he reached the grave. It was deserted, as he had expected at this time of night, and though he had tried his best to skirt the houses adjacent to the graveyard lest someone call the cops, he couldn't help but feel someone was watching.

There was scant illumination from the lightning, and Max was thankful for the darkness, making his secret job that much easier. Placing a small flashlight on the ground, he hefted his shovel and began to dig, taking one patch of freshly tilled soil from the ground after another. Max emptied the grave which he had just filled, aware of the lunacy of it all, constantly assuring himself that at the bottom he would find exactly what was to be expected, one very cold, very *dead*, Howard Broach. And then he would sleep. He would sleep the sleep of the dead, assured in the knowledge that there was no body after him.

But as he got closer and closer to unearthing what he fervently hoped would be a corpse, Max's uncertainty increased tenfold. And as he removed shovelful after shovelful of dirt where he was sure that he should be striking flesh, his uncertainty manifested into full-on terror, complete and abject horror, because the deeper he dug the more certain he became: there was no body.

Suddenly, he felt a hand upon his shoulder. Max could not even venture a scream as the hand forced him around to stand, face-to-leering-face, with the dead Howard Broach. *"MY RING!!!"* the dead man spat at him. Max was gripped by panic, unable to move, confronted by a man who should by all rights be lying in the cold ground. Max's mind reeled with the implications, the unreality of it all cascading over him.

A stroke of lightning split the stormy night sky, illuminating Howard in all his grizzly glory. The dead man did not hesitate, instead pushing Max, still clutching his shovel, into the grave. Howard followed, landing with a thud right next to him.

Max barely had time to sputter and choke, before he felt a four fingered hand pressing his face into the mud. Relying on nothing but instinct, Max seized a handful of earth in his hands, and in a quick motion ground the soil into Howard's eyes. Not pausing to think, seizing the opportunity, Max grabbed the shovel and swung. He connected, the blow smashing the side of Howard's head with the sharp trowel blade. And then as quickly as it had begun, it was over.

Howard didn't move. But that wasn't enough for Max, not nearly enough. Howard had been dead once before. Max had to be *sure* this time, so he brought the shovel down, again and again, striking with unrelenting fury. He didn't stop. Like a man possessed, he pounded Howard's corpse into oblivion.

Lost in his rage, Max almost didn't notice the voice of someone approaching. And even when he did, it took him a minute to pin down the sullen oaths and repetitious swearing, but as soon as he realized just what was going on, he scrambled from the hole. Taking a hiding place behind a weather-worn granite crypt, Max tightened the grip on the shovel. He had company.

✳ ✳ ✳

Max watched as the old man stood beside the hole with a somber look of bewilderment. It was clearly not what he expected to see. Putting it all together with the pick ax, saw, and shovel in the man's hand, Max chuckled, stepping out from his hiding place. "I know what you want, and its *mine*."

"What?... what?" The old man stammered, taking a step back.

"I know what you were trying to do. And I'm telling you, you're too late. I already got the ring."

"Max?! Is that you?"

"In the flesh." Max advanced on the startled man, his shovel held behind his back. "I'm sure you're a little surprised at seeing me here, huh, Uncle John?"

"Well... yes I was." He stalled for time, his hands reflexively grasping his pick-ax. "I got a call about a grave robbing."

"You call the cops on yourself? Is that it?" Max laughed at his own cleverness. "I know what you really want." He approached until they were both within striking distance. "You want *my ring*."

"It's my graveyard, my ring."

"I found it first." Max prepared for his swing. Just a little provocation and it would all be over. That was when he felt the hand. From the look on his uncle's face he could tell that the old man was likewise startled. However, that brief moment of surprise quickly turned into abject terror when realization struck, as cold clammy hands reached out from the grave, that utter chill and fear the last thing the pair felt as they were dragged down screaming into the earth.

The town sheriff was perplexed when he saw them. Two very dead gravediggers piled into what appeared to be a cemetery battleground. The lawman stared long and hard at those two familiar faces, now so horribly distorted in death, and thought. *I always wondered when those two would do each other in. Weren't too fond of each other.* Finally he shrugged impassively, telling himself to make a note of it. *Guess it's time to put out an ad for a new caretaker and grave digger.* With no further ado, the sheriff picked up the shovel. *County jobs,* he thought bitterly, and started the arduous task of filling in the grave.

House of Reflections

Karen tried her best to stifle the tears. She didn't know what her husband Kip would do if he saw her crying now, with all the witnesses, but she had a feeling that he wouldn't care who was looking and just wail off and belt her one in front of all the other people on the street. It wasn't anything about Kip that did it this time, but it was her son Stevie's words, so innocent, yet at the same time so cutting.

"Daddy, daddy! Can we go in, come on, can we? Please?!" Stevie Taylor was the textbook definition of an exuberant child. Short, bowl-cut blonde hair, with wide saucer eyes that seemed to take in everything about the world, and most importantly an insatiable curiously. Hearing her son call Kip that endearing term, "Daddy" was enough to rip apart what remained of Karen's heart, like a puppy tearing up a precious family heirloom, never knowing better. Karen was tempted to just scream, *Kip's not your daddy. John was your real daddy. Remember what a good person he was.* But it wasn't fear for herself that made her bite her tongue, it was fear for Stevie and for what Kip would do if he was reminded of Karen's past. She'd cried when she'd heard that Kip was insisting Stevie call him 'Dad' or some variation thereof, and the wound hadn't lost its sting.

Stevie was pointing at the Halloween Haunted House, the one decorated to delight young and old alike, complete with sprawling cobwebs, and recorded screams of those who had purportedly died inside playing from an unseen speaker. It was a dream for an overcurious child, and Stevie had been talking about it all week. He was tempted to repeat his plea, but he was old enough to know that to bug his stepfather would just as soon make Kip tell him "no" just to spite him.

After a moment of indecision, Kip finally grunted in irritation, making the decision for the three of them. "Fine, we'll go, if it'll shut you up." Kip was getting angry, as he had at least a dozen times today, one time becoming so ticked off that he'd cuffed the boy across the mouth to quiet him down. The man spat with disgust, looking at his wife with a glare that easily read, *why'd you have to have such a little brat?*

Kip, who'd spent years in prison, didn't look like a particularly mean man or abusive parent, if anything seeming effeminate and scrawny, but appearances were deceiving. His bespectacled, gaunt presence made him look like a professor or scholar, but the truth was Kip Watkins hadn't even graduated the seventh grade, taking a milling job when his father was murdered in the bed of another man's wife. Anyone who spent a good deal of time with Kip realized that beneath his prim appearance lay something *dark,* something *wrong.* Kip didn't consider himself to be a bad stepparent, but reasoned that sometimes kids just talked too much for their own good. "Well, go on now, Stevie," he gestured impatiently.

"Well…" There was a nervous look in Stevie's eye. He knew how his 'daddy' felt about sissies. But still, despite how desperately he wanted to go in the haunted house, Stevie just couldn't go in alone, it was just a little too scary. Maybe next year, when he was a little older, but not now. "Well… I was thinking we should all go in. You know, stick together."

Kip shot him an incredulous look as if to say he'd never seen so much of a baby in his entire life, but this time Karen spoke up, for them all. "That's a great idea. I think it would be fun." Kip looked at his wife with marked distain at having his decision usurped, but Karen didn't blanch under the glare. It might cost her a few bruises when Kip got drunker, later on, but right now there was no way she was going to send her child in alone. Besides, there was something about the haunted house that struck her as creepy. The shattered windows and dark halls seemed to strike her as *off*. There was no other real way to describe it, but there was some kind of intangible feeling that made her skin prickle.

She found herself wishing for her late husband, John's, presence, a habit that was becoming an addiction, so that they could face whatever was there, real or imagined, or anywhere else for that matter, together. Now, besides Stevie, all she had was Kip, the only family she'd had for several years, but she certainly couldn't voice her misgivings to him. *John would have said forget the whole thing and let's go get some ice cream for Stevie,* but Karen stifled that line of thought. The more John entered her mind, the more likely she was to blurt out something about him and set Kip off in a rage, and that was the last thing she needed right now. But strangely, all she could focus her thoughts on were John's large protective hands that she'd always joked about being big enough to hold all the world's problems. The image wouldn't leave her head, and Karen knew she missed him more than she could ever express.

Karen had been lost in her reverie, but she could tell something was irking her husband. Stevie was spouting off about how excited he was, his glances impatiently shifting between the several people milling around and the haunted house that no one seemed to be going into. *Maybe they're getting the same bad feeling I am,* Karen thought, but the more current bad feelings resounded from what was going on between Stevie and Kip. Stevie was a vocal kid, something Kip had never liked, and with a bad hangover still grating on him, Karen knew that Stevie was jumping on Kip's nerves. Karen was about to say something to quiet her son, but her husband beat her to the punch. "Don't you ever shut your mouth? Never give me a damn second of peace, boy. Now shut it or I'll shut it for you." He reached his hand back as if to emphasize, but Stevie didn't need a second warning. He fell silent. Karen did too, hating herself for standing there and letting it all happen, but she'd taken the abuse for so long, she'd learned to live with the numbness that comes with resignation.

Stevie, however, was too delighted with the prospect of the haunted house to let the admonishment hurt him for long. The attraction sat before them like a dark blight against a setting sun sky, standing nearly empty, yet somehow inviting. Some of the paint was peeling off the structure, showing the plywood and nails beneath, but to Stevie it was the singularly most frightening and most awe-inspiring sight he'd ever seen. Painted jet black, the weathered frame looked as if it could have been there for ages. *So real,* Stevie thought to himself as they made their approach.

* * *

"Three." Kip told the buxom girl at the ticket booth, his eyes slowly undressing her, while cringing over the three dollar fee, no doubt dreaming of how it would have bought him half of a six pack or a bottle of Wild Turkey. It had been Karen's idea to go to the haunted house because she was good friends with the owner, but Kip was still upset and didn't see why he had to go along. But in the end, Karen had been insistent, and it was her money, and as long as she was supporting Kip, she at least had some clout. She had wanted it to be a nice family day.

"So you're Kip?" The ticket girl asked.

"Yeah, what's it to ya?" Kip retorted sharply.

"Well, the owner said to let you in free for a private show."

"You hear that, Mom?" Stevie said, a slight glimmer in his eyes, as he looked at her, but Karen didn't share her son's mirth, instead actually becoming a little perplexed. What was this about a free private show? She knew the owner, an old friend she used to work with, but when she'd talked to him this morning he'd mentioned nothing about a free private show. And her tremor of fear escalated when she saw this girl at the booth, who was smiling lewdly at her husband claiming to know them both. Something wasn't adding up, but Stevie was already dragging her along, and Kip was fortifying himself with a sip from his trusty flask, so she had little choice but to go along. They found themselves approaching the haunted house, bathing in the overwhelming magnetic realism of the setting. Strangely, thoughts of the ticket woman began to fade, and then as they made it up the steps, Karen had almost forgotten her entire panic. By the time they were inside, she couldn't even remember seeing any woman at all.

* * *

Karen's first thought was, *God, if only John was here to see this.* Her husband had been a huge fan of the horror genre. As they entered the house the scary nuances stood out for her with their realism. A sign bearing the name "House of Reflections" was scrawled in very authentic looking blood above the entryway, and tenuous webs that easily could have been spun by a spider stuck in their mouths as they went, causing all involved to spit and sputter. There was a doorman, a teenager, shouting loudly, "Be wary! Beware!" Karen could see Kip resisting the urge to say something stupid, like telling the teen that he was the one who people needed to beware of. The chuckling laughter followed even as they traversed deep into the dank depths of the ghostly attraction.

Suddenly, it was pitch black, the only illumination coming from the few torches that hung from cobwebbed sconces lining the wall. The place smelled damp and earthen. Stevie savored every second of it, taking in every sight, every sound, every smell, and loving it.

Karen watched her son carefully, wary of any sudden movement, her nerves setting her on edge. *Why are you so scared?* she asked herself. *It's not like anything here can hurt you.* She tried to ally her fears but for some reason found she couldn't, not entirely. Her husband was obviously not enjoying himself, every now and then nipping at his stash of booze as they traversed deeper into the belly of the beast. Here and there they saw metal cages striped with pieces of supposed flesh, torture racks, and iron maidens from the Middle Ages. Amazingly, they all looked eerily authentic.

Where did they get this stuff? Karen wondered, again thinking of just how much her deceased husband, John, would have enjoyed taking this tour. And thinking too just how much safer she'd have felt. *Kip would probably take off running at the first sign of danger.* Glancing around, seeing vaulting ceilings that seemed impossibly too high for the building as they entered a new room, the thought gave her more of a chill, pondering just how scared she'd be to be left down here by herself. *God, I'm glad I didn't let Stevie in here alone.* Karen made a mental note to give her friend, the owner, a good talking to about his 'private tour', wishing desperately that there were other people with them, or at least nearby. Somehow, the absence of other human beings was the most frightening thing of all.

They soon entered a brighter room, a maze of mirrors, those funhouse staples, with their wacky reflections, some big and tall, some twisted and some small. Karen looked into one that gave a fairly accurate reflection and sighed. *I'm still reasonably pretty,* she thought to herself, despite the dark circles under her eyes. Looking at her abusive ball and chain beside her, again taking a sip from his flask, she wondered, *How the hell did I wind up with this loser?* But she knew the answer. Kip had seen her as a woman who was hurting from the death of her beloved husband and figured he could walk all over her. He put on a good show, seeming to be sensitive, empathetic, an ambitious guy who was going places. Every woman's dream. And then the ring had slipped on her finger, and as cliché as it sounded, that was the beginning of the end. She was probably one of the only brides in history, she had thought at the time, that cried on her wedding night. Looking down on the only thing that kept her going, she saw her son exhibiting that playful exuberance that always made her smile.

Stevie was currently engrossed with staring at a reflection of just how he would look if he was seven feet tall with arms the length of an chimpanzee. Kip noticed his stepson's behavior and said, "Hey, quit hoppin' around like a stupid ape." Stevie turned and looked at his stepfather with sadness on his face, giving Karen a stabbing pain in her heart. Below Stevie's left eye was the beginnings of purple-black bruise, a souvenir from a few nights earlier when Stevie had accidentally knocked over a stack of 'Daddy's' precious magazines. Karen had been nearly unconscious from a beating sustained after coming home too late from work to prepare dinner. Kip had already been very, very drunk. The next morning, Karen had almost taken her kitchen utensils and plunged them into Kip's passed out body, but in the end, fear had stayed her hand. Fear of what would happen if she couldn't finish the job, and the even greater uncertainty of incarceration leaving Stevie with no one, all other family dead and gone.

"Sorry, what was that?" Stevie had been speaking, but Karen had been too lost in her own world to have picked it up.

"I said, 'where are we?'" For the first time since they'd entered the haunted house Karen noticed an emotion on Stevie's face that wasn't excitement or joy. It was fear.

"We're right..." She looked left and saw only a vacant hall stretching off into nothingness, and to her right, the same, the distortion of the mirrors making it impossible to tell the real exit from the millions of fake ones. "You know, I really don't know." Karen felt a slight chill as she gave voice to the words. Kip looked pissed, ready to lash out given any provocation, and Karen's sense of fear grew tenfold. Something was definitely wrong here. Confusion milled among them as a powerful voice split the oppressive silence.

"Welcome Kip, it's reckoning time." The voice was seething with anger, yet to Karen it seemed somehow familiar.

"Oh yeah?" Kip turned, his hatred temporarily displacing onto whatever had the audacity to interrupt him. He glanced around, seeing nothing but his own reflection refracted a hundred different ways, from fat to skinny, short to shorter. Angered with nothing to lash out at, he became even more enraged. Turning back to Karen, he shouted, "You stupid bitch, it was *your* friend who set this up. What do you think I am, an ignoramus?"

Karen cringed as Kip approached. She knew that when he used big words like ignoramus, trying to make himself feel smart, he was ready for a fight.

"You know I didn't mean that…" Karen's words were cut off as Kip struck her, hard, across the mouth, knocking her to the ground. Karen's head swam, but Kip didn't stop kicking her in the side as she lay there. Stevie came to his mom's side, placing himself between Kip and the object of his wrath. The stepfather didn't hesitate, backhanding the boy and sending him sprawling.

The voice came again, frothing with rage. "Why don't you try that on me?!"

Kip turned to the void of mirrors, feeling like the heavyweight champion of the world. "Why don't you show yourself, punk, if you got the stones, and see just what I'm going to do to you?!"

Suddenly, like a ghost, a clown stepped from the shadows. But in reality, the mirrors made it look like a thousand clowns stepping forth in suits of red, with white stripes running down one side, and a patch blue stars across the chest. "Okay. Here I am. Why don't you say that to my face?" Karen was dazed, on the edge of consciousness, but through the haze of clown makeup, the figure looked comfortingly familiar. To Kip, however, the apparition was a just new target to hurl his anger at. The clown was dressed like an ordinary circus performer, appearing bright, vibrant, but with makeup that seemed to shimmer, and a body that looked almost transparent. Seeing this wispy form, Kip smiled. It looked like it would be a one-sided battle. Still, there was something oddly fiery in the clown's eyes, something *knowing*.

"You think I'm scared of *you*, Bozo?! You'll get yours right now!" Kip charged forward, a headlong bull rush from his younger days of back-alley football. He stopped dead in his tracks after ten paces when the saw the clown up close, its willowy form showing the mirrors beyond, but its grasping hands looking all too tangible, and powerful.

Instantly, Kip turned and ran, fleeing from this obviously crazed clown, pushing right past Stevie as he went by. The frightened boy was quick on his heels, scared to leave his mother, but knowing that in her condition there was nothing he could do to protect her by staying. He decided it would be better to lead the creature away from his mother. Karen watched them go through her haze of near-unconsciousness and lifted a hand warily, before her injuries dropped her back to the ground. There was nothing she could do but wait, and pray. *John why did you have to leave us...?*

✳ ✳ ✳

The clown was just behind Kip and Stevie, its wrath seemingly focused on the angry stepfather. Soon the hunted pair found themselves lost in the huge hall of mirrors, unable to get out, the white face and cold blue eyes of the approaching killer clown just steps behind.

Kip and Stevie ran with all their might, ducking and dodging behind the mirrors, everywhere they turned, seeing that grinning painted face. Suddenly, Stevie was thrown to the ground, Kip's foot sending the young child sprawling, thinking that a small sacrifice could give him the time he needed to get out of there. Stevie, infinitely hurt by his stepfather's actions, could scarcely move, hatred and sadness burning in his sweet innocent eyes. Still the clown crept closer, seeming to be everywhere, in every mirror, in every reflection, all around. Finally, Stevie forced his unwilling legs to move, getting up and taking off once again. The clown was definitely closer now; he could feel it. Stevie painfully watched as Kip abandoned him, ducking into a niche between two mirrors, leaving Stevie to the clutches of the clown.

Hoping that there had been some mistake, that his stepfather would somehow protect him, Stevie ran to where Kip crouched. The boy would have had better luck running in front of a firing squad. Kip screamed out, "What are you doing, you idiot?!" his voice frantic with panic. "You fool, now we're both dead." Almost as if summoned by his words, the mirror behind the pair shattered revealing the chalk-white face of the clown. In one swift motion, the giant hands came down, smashing into Kip, dropping him to the ground, where he lay clutching his broken bones, crying. Stevie was petrified, unable to move, unable to even scream for help.

Thin runnels of blood were already seeping from Kip's wounds. The clown hovered atop them both and seemed to smile sadly, a large hand coming down, clamping Kip's face tight, and squeezing, like getting juice from an orange. "Last chance at redemption." Kip looked up at eyes that seemed to waver in the faint light, wondering, if this clown was really a ghost or something worse. There was no tremor of fear in the clown's voice when it asked, "You or the boy? One lives, one dies. Your choice."

Kip didn't hesitate. "The boy." The clown reached down and grabbed Stevie's hand, pushing him back towards the emergency exit.

"No!" Kip screamed, seeing his chance of survival running out the haunted house door. "I meant *kill* the boy."

The clown shuddered, and with a fury that rivaled hell's own, crushed Kip's throat with a sickening gurgle. "Wrong answer! I already knew what you'd say, but I had to give you a chance. Like everything else in your life, Kip, you failed." The clown screamed, angry cries mixed with tears of sorrow. As Kip faded away, he could hear something faint, but something that made him angry,

angry at himself, angry at his wife, and most of all angry at Stevie. But none of that mattered now. It was all over now, at least for him. Realization struck. The last thing Kip heard was a clown voice calling after Stevie saying, "Remember I'll always love you." With that Kip faded into oblivion.

*   *   *

Karen was crying. Something that was becoming all too common place, the mirrors showing a resounding panorama like the same television show playing on a thousand screens at once, and Karen felt sickened by it. Stevie was gone. Her one reason for living. Kip was gone, abandoning her as she had always known he one day would. But that was to be expected. And now, sitting in the dank hall of mirrors, waiting for that monster with the familiar voice to come finish the job, she just couldn't help but wonder what had happened. *Why did you abandon us?* She thought to herself and to no one in particular. It was easy to sink into despair. She was desperately tying to get up, her chest feeling really tight, some ribs definitely cracked if not broken, when the familiar voice came back to her.

Her vision was still hazy, but she didn't know if it was a clown this time. She couldn't tell exactly what it was. Karen shrank back, then, something inside her saying that she'd lived in fear long enough, forced her to get to her knees, trying to stand. If she had to go, she wasn't going out lying down, she'd had enough of that.

The voice came, dreamlike, and comforting, "I didn't abandon you by choice. It was just my time to go." Karen felt the warmth of large, gentle hands lifting her, and suddenly she was up, the pain in her ribs gone. "You're going to be fine now." She felt the presence all around her, realization striking her, and bringing fresh tears, though ones of a different kind. She couldn't see it, exactly, but the familiar presence was there all the same, like a nimbus of light encircling her, leading her up and out. John. At first, she'd wondered why he had appeared as a clown, and then it came to her in a flash. Stevie's second birthday. They hadn't been able to afford a clown and John had dressed the part, delighting their son and bringing tears to Karen's eyes.

"Is it over?" After all the years, after all the questions she had wanted to ask, Karen found that this was the best that she could do.

The voice hesitated. The question was a relative one. "Yes. For you, it's a new beginning. Stevie is fine and you can start over." There was a pause as Karen felt herself being led from the hall of mirrors. An emergency exit door lay just ahead. "I can't stay much longer Karen, and Stevie is waiting for you. But as to your question, know that I'll be waiting, and it's never over." Karen could only smile, a trickle of a tear draining down one cheek, yearning just to touch him one more time. "You have to go now, Karen. You have to go."

The door opened, and Karen stepped through, wanting one last look, and saying, "I love you," as she did.

"I love you too, Karen. Always." The warmth carried her even as she made her exit, Stevie standing there staring, the day filled with promise.

"I love you, too," the voice came one last time, as the haunted house door swung shut on a place of remembered dreams and memories.

Body Bag

His wife was in the bag, well, what was left of her. Vincent had been able to get rid of one of the hands when he'd stopped for gas, providing a very hungry and very scrawny dog with a decent meal, and he knew that if he could just make it to Forester City, he'd be in the clear. His brother, Trevor, an undertaker, would burn up the leftovers in the crematorium oven, and then he'd be home free. Being the close brother that he was, Trevor was more than willing to help, especially knowing what that wretched wife had done to little Timmy.

Just as Vincent's blood was beginning to boil, the thought of what his wife had done making his skin blister, he heard the squeal of tires approaching from behind. His own car had broken down a few miles back, and a brief look under the hood confirmed the fact that the engine had finally died once and for all, the wife having always insisted any money saved for a transmission overhaul be spent on herself instead. With at least another thirty miles to go until he reached Forester City, Vincent stuck out his thumb, hoping to herald a ride, knowing that the sooner he disposed of his wife's body, the better. It was only too late that he realized, his thumb sticking out like a homing beacon, the runnel of dust settling and the tires screeching to a halt, that he'd flagged down a county sheriff.

Just my luck, he thought bitterly, cursing everything that had brought him to this point. The car that had broken down, the person who he'd decided to spend his life with who'd destroyed everything he'd ever loved. Standing there, Vincent just wished he could go back in time, before the nightmare that had become his life. Back to when Timmy was still alive, when they were struggling, but surviving, in Jamestown, a place he could never return to again. It seemed to Vincent that life wasn't without a terrible sense of irony, because the cop's car that pulled up next to him bore the blazing insignia of the Jamestown County Sheriffs. *Figures,* Vincent thought. He'd only made it three cities away from home before the car died, unfortunately still within county lines. But the whole situation still made him seethe. It just wasn't fair.

"How y'all doin'?" the cop asked as he exited the car. "Awful hot out to be walkin', ain't it?" He was a burly man with a broad-brimmed cowboy hat that didn't seem to be doing its job, judging from the large lobster-red sunburn beneath both eyes. Now that the cop mentioned it, Vincent realized just how hot it really was. He was sweating profusely, and he prayed the sheriff didn't take that for a sign of guilt.

"Uh, I'm fine, actually. Just doin' a bit of travelin.'" Vincent spoke with that same southern drawl the sheriff did. Having grown up and spent his entire life in Dixieland, it was as much a part of him as a love of grits and jazz, but the officer's inflection was far more pronounced, a good old boy if Vincent had ever seen one.

"Well, now, that's a relief. See, I thought you was in some trouble. Need a lift?" It was one simple question that put Vincent in one hell of a situation. If he accepted the ride, it was almost certain the cop would find out he had a body in the bag. But if he refused, especially after flagging the officer down, then it was almost certain that he'd be detained and searched, and that was completely out of the question.

It was a lose-lose situation, but Vincent figured that given the choice, he might as well spend the his time in the cool air-conditioned confines of a police car, rather than sprawled spread eagle along the side of a dusty road. He gauged his chances of making a run for it and realized the futility. There was nowhere to go. Trying to keep the fear from his voice, Vincent smiled, "Appreciate it."

"Good. Could use a little company. Been investigatin' all mornin' and I jus' want a li'l human company to brighten my day. I saw a car a couple miles back, a clunker stashed off to the side of the road. That wouldn't be yers, now would it?"

Not knowing exactly what the cop knew, but hoping his plates hadn't been run, as he was probably the prime suspect in the disappearance of his wife, Vincent effected an air of nonchalance. "Nope. No car. Just out fer a li'l walkin' trip." The officer stared at him through reflective lenses, but said nothing. Vincent tried not to let the cop have any more time for questions as he scurried around the backside of the patrol car, hoping to drop the body as soon as possible. "Could ya pop the trunk?"

Vincent swallowed hard when he heard the officer's response, "Oh, here, I'll take that bag fer ya."

Vincent's stomach knotted, each footfall of the officer's seeming impossibly slow, realizing that it was the beginning of the end. And as the officer unlocked the trunk, Vincent was sure that the cop could smell the decomposition of his wife's body, could just feel that horrid offal stench pervading his nostrils, offending every olfactory sense. But the officer said nothing and merely took the bag and tossed it in the trunk. Vincent could barely believe it, expecting at any second to feel the sting of handcuffs on his wrists, but the officer gave the bag no more than a second thought, slamming the trunk shut and getting into the car. Vincent, not wanting to press his luck or raise any more suspicion, hurried into the passenger seat as the cop fired up the engine.

After the initial question of Vincent's destination was answered, the two men drove for a few minutes in silence, the whole time the passenger convinced he could smell a permeable aura of death emanating form the trunk.

"Name's Zeek," the cop said, extending a meaty palm. Vincent took it quickly and shook it, praying that the cop wasn't sensing that same pungent odor he was now certain was filling the cabin of the car. "What's yours?"

"Mi..Micheal," he stammered.

"Mike, my boy, you don't know how good it is to be talkin' to another livin', breathin' soul. I've been investigatin' since early this mornin' an' I keep thinkin' I'm gonna go insane if'n I don't get some real human contact."

"So whatcha been investigatin'?" Vincent tried for anything that might divert the cop's attention away from questions about why his passenger had been walking along a deserted road carrying a suspicious looking package. Questions with no good answers. A sign in the distance provided a slight sliver of hope, "Forester City -

15 miles." Vincent knew if he could just keep Zeek's mind occupied for a few more minutes, he might be all right.

"Well, I was investigatin' a domestic call, back in Jamestown. Funny thing was, when I got there, wasn't no one home. But there was blood. Lots of it. Nowadays it's awful hard to prove someone's dead 'less we got a body, so that's what I'm on the troll fer. Car was gone too, and records say the missin' guy's got family in Forester City, so that's where I'm headed. And seems as if it's yer lucky day, now don't it, pardner?" Vincent couldn't help but cringe, his stomach churning, his hands growing clammier by the second. The cop was talking about him, there was no doubt about it. Zeek leaned in close, pulling off the reflective lenses as he did. "Y'all married?"

Vincent knew the end of the road when he saw it. This whole time, the cop had been toying with him. *Forester City. A clunker stashed off to the side of the road, that wouldn't be yers now would it?* The cop's words echoed in his head. *He'd known all along.* Vincent still felt trapped, suffocated, the rancid smell from the bag in the trunk filling the air with pungent aroma too strong to be ignored. Knowing that he was a goner anyway, Vincent still decided not to give an inch, but instead to play along until the final card was dealt. "I'm recently widowed." He grinned sardonically to himself.

Strangely, Zeek was all sympathy. "Sorry to hear that."

Vincent could have either laughed or cried, sometimes that border becoming blurred. "Well, that makes one of us." As the cop shot him a strange look, he continued. "She was the most horrible person I've ever known. I hope she rots in a river of darkness. Gave me misery ever since I slipped that ring on her finger. Ya know, I worked two jobs jus' to feed our family and it wasn't never enough. She always took it out on our son, real abusive. I don't have no education. Could only do what I could. Would've done anything for that woman, but it weren't ever good enough. Ever."

"What happened?"

"Well, you could say she just went to pieces." Vincent couldn't help but chuckle, wondering if this was what it was like to stand on the brink of madness.

"Huh. Ya know, you look real familiar, pardner," Zeek said with his own smile.

Those words. The curtain was about to be drawn, the game most certainly up, like a twisted version of Let's Make a Deal where the only prize left was Death Row. Vincent was about to open his mouth to admit his guilt, tired of the whole charade, when Zeek spoke again.

"Now, I know it. That's who y'all look like. My partner investigated a case 'bout a month back, I seen the pictures. It was a mother who drowned her own son, 'cause they couldn't afford fer all three of 'em. Pure evil, she was. But man, if'n y'all don't just look like that husband. Said he was workin' at the time but he was sure she'd drowned the boy. But with no witnesses, we had to rule it an accident, even though he had so many bruises. Poor li'l boy. Timmy was his name. I'll never forget it." Zeek smiled, but there was no humor in it. "That's mighty funny, seein' as how y'all look so much like that man, 'n it was that woman's disappearance I was investigatin.'"

Just get it over with, Vincent thought bitterly, the whole time feeling like he could just drift away, float off to somewhere peaceful where values were still held and things still made sense. The unreality seemed to sweep him up in its grasp.

Zeek continued on, as if nothin' was wrong. "But ya know what? If'n that husband ya look like had decided to get rid of that monster, I wouldn't be blamin' him one bit. I had a sister murdered 'bout fifteen years ago. Beautiful girl, killed by a drifter. She's the reason I became a cop. Never did catch the guy, he's still out there somewheres, but I'm watchin' fer him, always. My sister's with Jesus now, I know that sure as I know the sky's blue, but I tell y'all, much as I hate to admit it, even after all these years I'd give anything just to see the look in that bastard's eyes as I squeezed the life outta him. I know what that man felt like losing his son and I feel mighty sorry for him, but I wouldn't wanna be in his shoes. We got an eye out for him. We gotta nab him 'n bring him in, much as most of us don't want to. The law, ya know?"

Vincent hated the way Zeek was beating around the bush. *Yeah, great, y'all feel sorry for me. I'll think about that as I gather dust in a cell awaitin' my execution. Just do it already,* he nearly screamed within his own mind, *just slap on the cuffs and take me in. No more tauntin', no more tormentin'.* The smell of rotting flesh assailed his senses once again, seeming as if the cabin of the car had become filled with the oppressive stench of decomposition. The silence hung between them like a shroud.

"Well, here we are. I gotta go talk to the husband's brother," Zeek said with a grin, as he pulled to the side of the road. Vincent could see the funeral home in the distance outside his window, just past the meandering Muddy River that ran deep throughout the county. *So this is where it'll happen. This is where he's gonna get me, just a few feet from freedom.* He could almost taste the irony, bitter on the back of his tongue. But as Zeek opened the door and popped the trunk, Vincent didn't feel the sting of handcuffs being clenched down upon his wrists.

And as the cop handed over that bag, Vincent was sure that this was the coup de gras, to be the caught with bag in hand. Zeek merely smiled sadly and said, "Thanks fer the company." And even as a drop of blood fell from the bag, landing between them, Zeek didn't seem to notice, leaving Vincent in the road, no cuffs, no questions asked.

*　*　*

As he walked away, waving all the while, Vincent could hear Zeek's parting words, ones which he took to heart. "Ya know, I think drowin' the bones in the Muddy River would be fittin'. And seein' as we already dredged it this mornin', I don't think nobody'll be lookin' there again. Just some advice, now. Take care, *Vincent*."

And as Vincent stood there on the side of the road under the sun's bright rays, the promise of a new day and a new start at hand, he gave a little prayer of thanks for everything that had happened and thanks that he had been fortunate enough to be left holding the bag.

A Long Drop
and a Short Stop

Victor, for the life of him, couldn't figure out how he'd gotten there. It was as if he'd been catapulted into some strange parallel universe with no recollection of how it happened, everything an amnesiac blur in his mind. But the worst part was, despite the uncanny oddness of his situation, Victor seemed to know this place. His surroundings resembled his old hometown so closely that, for a second, he was sure he was back in Kansas. Tears welled in his eyes as he took it all in. There was Peter's Pharmacy and Old Man Kelly's Taxidermy standing juxtaposed in the still night air, and the city park, which had played host to so many town events throughout the years, stretching out before him. Victor, though, in spite of the disturbing peculiarity of it all, felt truly at home, at peace. It was only after looking around curiously that a real sense of disquiet began to set in.

"Where the hell am I?" Victor said beneath his breath as he surveyed the town square, trying to pinpoint the source of his unease. The windows of Peter's Pharmacy were dark, but that wasn't all that odd, as night had fallen. Still, something didn't set right. Taking a closer look, Vincent could see the utter blackness beyond the windows, suggesting more of a complete vacancy, an absence of being, rather than just the lights out for the night. Victor gazed upon the thick strands of cobwebs lining the windows of the taxidermy shop and shuddered, thinking of the army of arachnids that must have spun the intricate tapestry. Even the town square itself seemed empty and foreboding. No sound filled the air, not the faint hum of grasshoppers chirping a late-night song or a slight breeze bleating out atmospheric ambiance. There was nothing.

No, not nothing, Victor thought, listening closer, hearing a faint trickle of sound that somehow seemed to be coming more from within his own mind than any other source. It was only a whisper of noise, half-caught, like snippets of conversation heard from a broken radio, but the words were ominous, '...*willfully and maliciously... death...*" and their grim portent made Victor shiver. A part of him wondered if this was the first stage of insanity. *They always hear voices,* he thought and then shook his head. As quickly as the words had come, they vanished, leaving Victor wondering if he'd even heard them at all. *Probably my mind playing tricks on me,* he thought bitterly as he began to walk forward, deeper into the town, wanting to leave the city park and its sinister solitude behind.

Despite the streetlights, everything seemed impossibly dark. Victor turned from Creek Street to Owl Road and continued on, wishing he could escape this nightmare of a town, desperately hoping that it was all just a dream. He felt as if he was suffocating, the whole thing seeming impossible, the unthinkable reality of awakening only to find that he was the last person alive. Thoughts along those lines stopped abruptly as he took another corner, coming face-to-face with a very tired and haggard-looking old man.

The relief Victor felt, knowing he was no longer alone, was dashed instantly as the stranger spoke, "Hey Victor, you miss me?" The elderly man, who was dressed in a beggar's rags, chuckled, a hysterical tinge to his laughter. Victor took a step back as the wizened man moved closer. "Oh, come on now, you couldn't have forgotten me. Not after everything we've been through."

The beggar's dark-rimmed eyes, deep-set into sunken sockets, fixed him with a stern look. It took Victor a minute, but he realized he really *did* know the old panhandler. The recognition, though, only made Victor more terrified and he retreated a step further. "Mr. Jones, is that... is that you? But, how?"

The beggar laughed again, this time fiercer and harder, and Victor could see flecks of blood on the man's lips as he spoke. "Well, after Johnny was killed, I didn't have anyone to help me with the shop so I lost my store." The recollection of Mr. Jones' old candy shop tugged hard at Victor's heartstrings. It was a place where he'd spent many summer days when he was a kid. Victor didn't have time for remembrance as the man continued on, "I was grieving so hard... and, well, I got TB, and I guess now that'll take me away, too. But that won't really be so bad, now will it?" Mr. Jones fixed Victor with a glare that was penetrating, *knowing*, and suddenly Victor felt very, very afraid.

Turning quickly, wanting nothing more to do with this strange place or its inhabitants, Victor took off running. The darkness seemed to increase as he went and he could once again feel the cool sting of tears in his eyes. Victor took one corner and then another, finding himself on Paradise street. A bright light split the darkness in the distance and Victor ran to it, hoping it was some miraculous way out, a gateway home or something of the like. Only as Victor drew closer did he realize that the glow he saw wasn't some portal, but merely the illumination cast from an overly-bright street lamp. Two seconds later Victor noticed the silhouette of shadow in the ray of light, and he looked up. That was when Victor saw it, hanging from the crosspiece of the light. "There's no way..." Up above him, suspended by a noose, hung a corpse, swaying in the still night air.

Like everything else about this strange place, the dead body was all too-familiar. "Gerald?" Victor asked, and even as he spoke, he found himself shocked to see the body shaking, the corpse's eyes opening and fixing him with a harsh, condemning glare.

"...Strung me up and left me to die..." came an accusatory voice, but Victor refused to listen, once again continuing his frantic running.

Within a few short turns, Victor found himself back in the town square. "What the hell..." he said, exasperated, his terror magnifying as he realized the town square, which had been so dead, was now alive with activity. The carefully groomed grass was being torn asunder by hands pawing their way up from the dirt. The vengeful eyes and screaming mouths of corpses emerged from the ground, broken fingernails clawing their way free. Victor had seen this same scene many times on the silver screen, the dead once again coming back to life, but, unlike the movies, this was really happening.

Six bodies, riddled and marred with various gunshot wounds emerged from the Earth and immediately they headed in Victor's direction. He recognized one of them as Johnny, the beggar's son, and instantly the truth of what was transpiring struck him like a freight train coming at full force. Victor felt paralyzed, his memory returning to him and the horror of it freezing him dead in his tracks. Johnny spoke up, sounding eerily like the snippet of sound he'd heard earlier, '...*and for the malicious and unrepentant crime of eight counts of first degree murder...*" Victor shivered, feeling the weight of the corpses' gazes upon him.

    Victor turned away, only to see the most familiar face he'd seen in this horrible place staring back at him. "Best friends forever, right?" came a recognizable voice. There was a smile on the man's face that was both sad and malicious, and then the person who had been Victor's closet buddy for years spoke again, "...*and for those crimes Victor Abrams Johnson, your sentence is death...*" Victor didn't even had time to respond as cold hands seized him, gripping tight. Victor screamed as he was dragged into the ground, but despite the terror, he knew, deep down, that he was truly home.

"Oh God," one of the witnesses said with a kind of reverence.

"I know," another said, "Didn't show any kind of repentance or remorse, even at the end." The two men stared at the dead man's feet which had ceased to kick a few seconds before. It had not been a clean fall.

"A long drop and a short stop is usually enough to make even the most callous bastard rethink their ways," the first one said, feeling the melancholy vindication that was commonplace in the aftermath of execution.

"Yeah, but a guy who can gun down seven of his closest friends in cold blood after hanging Gerald, well, that takes a certain kind of sickness," the other replied.

"And don't forget Johnny."

"Don't worry, Mr. Jones, I'll never forget your son." They sat there for a second, even as the sheriffs began to usher people out of the execution viewing room. "It's so that strange. You can know someone like Victor for years and then one day they just snap. Sometimes I think that he had that craziness in him for a long time and we just didn't recognize it until it was too late. But I think that maybe what Shirley Jackson said about houses fits people too. Some of them are just born bad."

Mr. Jones just sat there for a second before picking up his cane. "I don't know, I really don't. But I don't think anyone is beyond salvation if they ask for it."

"Yeah," the other man said solemnly, "but you just said it. It's a matter of asking for it." Neither said another word as they made their way out of a place of death, feeling like they were carrying a piece of it with them as they went, but knowing, that at least now, some things could be put to rest.

An Unseen Stranger

William Jacobs put the newspaper down and tried his best to keep his hands from shaking. He knew he was running late and this was the last thing he needed right now, his pounding heart unable to control its incessant throb. Thinking of the words he'd just read, so personal and terrifying, the tremors in his fingers returned. He could practically feel the full onset of his hangover, gnawing at him, and William thought he might be sick. Re-reading the newspaper, he found, as he had the last two times he did so, that the words were perfectly normal. *Two Slain in New York Streets: No Leads at This Time.* But it didn't do his nerves any good. William knew what he had seen.

The morning had started off like any other, an extra long shower to combat the after effects of a long night of drinking. With barely the time for a cup of coffee, it was the glance at the morning paper that halted William dead in his tracks. What he saw caused him to drop his mug in shock, the words greeting him ominously as he held the newsprint closer to make sure what he was seeing was true. The bold headline had read: *William Jacobs Slain in New York Streets: William Bleeds This Time.* He'd rubbed his eyes when he read it, thinking he was still half-asleep or in the wake of some crazy dream, but the words were still there. It was only when his frantic hands were dialing 911 and the paper fell to the floor, that a different headline appeared. Fear's icy hands clutched his stomach as William refolded the paper, setting it down and picking it back up, trying to make the horrible words reappear. But they wouldn't come.

The clock read half past six and William tried to assure himself he was just overworked and stressed. It was a reasonable self-deceiving excuse, made even more believable by the fact that there was no longer any tangible proof to the contrary. The impact of the words, however, followed the young lawyer as he walked out the door, taking extra care to double lock it behind him, thinking the whole time, *William Bleeds This Time.*

✳ ✳ ✳

The subway was nearly deserted and the familiar solitude of the early morning transit was already beginning to set William's mind at ease. He had started to write off the whole ordeal as the delusions born of waking up too early with not enough sleep and too much liquor in his system. He wondered absently if this was what *delirium tremens* felt like.

The incandescent glow of flickering platform signs bathed the car in their eerie glow and William felt a shiver beneath his coat, the words returning to him even as he tried to force them out. He looked out the window in an attempt to keep his mind off the ominous portent of this morning's news, taking in the curves of his face in the reflection as he gazed at the kaleidoscopic colors of the underground.

The exit for Times Square flew by, followed by 112th and others, as the outside world began to blur and William started drift off. *God, I need more rest,* he thought to himself, knowing just what this morning's ordeal was going to do to his already bad sleep patterns. *And just when that shrink says I'm starting to get over the paranoia...* His thoughts were cut off in an instant as he caught sight of something out the window. It came and went in a flash, a mere glimpse out of the corner of the eye amid the confusion of the passing subway tunnel. The afterimage, though, lingered far longer in William's eyes, and recognition of what he had seen was unmistakable. It was a face. He hadn't seen it clear enough to make it out completely, but there was something about the leering projection that made William's stomach quiver. And what made it even worse was that William knew from his long experience with the subway system that there was no way anyone on a platform could have looked so distinct or been that *close*. Images of the Twilight Zone episode came to mind, the one where only one person knew there was a monster tearing the airplane apart and no one believed him. What made things even more chilling was that the face William saw wasn't that of a complete stranger, it was one that looked, somehow, familiar.

I'm losing it, William thought, wondering if people who really did go insane were lucid enough to realize it. He didn't think so. Not wanting to chance another voyeuristic vision outside the window, William turned his attention back to his immediate surroundings. As soon as he did, he found himself face-to-leering-face with a transient, one who looked as if he *really* had lost it. Spittle hung through days of unshaven stubble, and when the man spoke, William could almost taste the words on his breath.

"You're going to die, oh yes you are. You're going to be screaming. You're going to be beggin' for it to end, William. But you know what? It'll never end, Hot Shot, not 'till you're dead. Bet you didn't see that comin' did ya? Even after all your pleadin'. You're going to die for what you did!" The transient was yelling by this point. William pushed the man aside, fiercely, feeling the frantic need to get as far away as he could, rushing to the door. Luck seemed to be on his side, temporarily, as the train pulled into a station. William didn't hesitate, rushing off the train, still miles from his intended stop, knowing he'd have to catch a cab. But it was enough just to be away from the lunatic bum. It was only after the doors had swung shut and he was heading up out of the terminal that William realized the man on the train had called him by name.

* * *

William fortified himself with two more cups of strong coffee, made stronger still by four fingers of whisky. He tried not to drink in the mornings anymore, not wanting to do anything that classified him as an alcoholic, but today had been a worthy exception.

William had already come to the conclusion that he would tell no one. He knew that nobody would believe him, and they would probably chalk it up to post-traumatic stress. No one would blame him for having visions after the ordeal he'd been through five years earlier, but that didn't mean they'd believe him. *I don't even know if I believe it myself,* he added. But as hard as William tried, he found he couldn't deny the fact that there had been a face outside his window or the eerie way in which the homeless stranger had known his name. *Maybe it was the DTs,* he thought repeatedly, *I've heard crazy things like this happen,* and by the time lunch rolled around he had himself almost believing it.

He was on his way to the commissary, walking down the hall from his opulent office, when he stopped abruptly. It was almost like a compulsive force that caused him to pause in his step, his eyes drawn to the names etched on the firm's somber memorial plaque, hung so ceremoniously in a place of honor. It seemed strange that so many employees had died. After all, this wasn't the Army or CIA. Thinking of all the lawyers and workers who had died tragically sent an ill feeling of dread through William's entire body. *Guilt,* he thought sullenly before moving on. *Everybody feels it,* he tried to tell himself as he finally wrenched his recalcitrant gaze from the plaque. William said nothing to the secretary as he passed, but just the same, he swore he could feel her eyes on him as he went, judging.

✳   ✳   ✳

It was waiting for him when he got back, sitting on his desk, in plain sight. William could see the outline of it through the window pane of his office as he approached. *No, that's just not possible.* William checked his door and found it locked, just as he had left it. As a partner in the law firm, he had his own office, and though he seldom locked the door, today he had taken no chances. And yet, inexplicably, there it was: a simple paper-filled folder, sitting atop his desk in a locked room. Even worse, William was pretty sure he knew which folder it was.

Calm down, he cautioned himself, *maybe you put it there for some reason before you left.* He unsuccessfully tried to rationalize the situation, drifting through a cloud of disbelief. It was the same sensation he'd felt when he'd seen the face on his subway ride, that sense of familiarity striking him, and it frightened William more than words could express. Somewhere deep inside himself, a chained down, drowned memory was starting to surface. He had known when he'd seen the face outside the subway window exactly what horror it was tied to, but he hadn't wanted to admit it at the time. Now it looked like he would have no choice.

Digging out his keys, William turned the lock and hurried to his desk. He didn't even look at the case file, knowing deep down just which one it would be, before he snatched it up and heaved it into the trash. Pulling out a monogrammed lighter he'd received when he'd been made junior partner, William flicked up a flame and tossed it in. The papers coiled and curdled as they burned, a plume of black smoke creating a slight haze in the office. *Still better than facing that,* William thought, leaning back in his chair, fanning the smoke, taking a few sips from his ever-present flask, trying to recapture his dying buzz, and forget the whole terrible ordeal. But he found the job far too difficult. He couldn't keep his mind off the smoldering file, the people and situation it represented, a mixture of fear and the elation filling him, as it always did, when he thought of *that* case. The aftermath of that trial and verdict was solely responsible for William Jacobs being named the youngest partner in the firm's illustrious history, creating the cause for the mixture of joy and dread.

Even as the fire died down to a slow burn, the thoughts lingered, and so did the guilt. William didn't even notice, as he slipped into restless sleep in his chair, that through the smoke, still visible in the ashes, was the slightly recognizable manila tab reading *Hillman Case File,* the words blackened and charred like some old newsprint.

✳   ✳   ✳

He walked to the sink and put the Drano back. It would be too painful that way, the tears already streaming down his face. He couldn't remember the last time he'd shaved, and the cracked mirror showed a shell of a man.

Blood dripped down his wrists, the tile of the floor already soaked, causing the need for caution, for fear of falling and breaking something. The thought made him laugh, a manic quality festering in it. In a sudden fit of rage he lashed out, smashing the mirror into shards, taking one and digging into his forearm, the amount of blood obscene. Pictures strewn across the counter, now wrinkled with tears and other fouler substances, as a used up joint, crack pipe, and syringe all laid in good company in an ashtray from Walmart. He'd tried to OD and found it harder than he'd expected. He'd wondered how so many rock stars were able to perfect the art. Falling into the tub, his legs becoming weaker now, from blood loss, the man who would soon be a memory, prepared his final statement, hoping it wouldn't be so mired with blood that it would be illegible. The scratch marks on the paper were bad enough, where he had crossed and then re-crossed out names. There was only one name left. One he hadn't been able to get. The police would no doubt be there soon, and the man, through bitter tears, thought of how he would be remembered. A maniac, a psychotic, they would say, never knowing the real story. He thought of beautiful things, feeling the cool steel of his final exit pressing up against his skin. He thought of his wife. His ex now, but not in his head. He thought about his daughter with warmth, even after all she'd done, forgiving her for being so easily manipulated. He thought about the plush office and how he'd lost it all. And he thought about one last thing, one last nagging detail, that would not let him rest, and that was, despite all the planning, he hadn't been able to finish the job, not completely. And now he'd be branded a killer, added to the long list of lies and untruths. Abusive Spouse. Molester. Killer. Thoughts of revenge, and more of regret filling his mind until he couldn't take it any longer, and then the bullet slammed into his brain.

✳   ✳   ✳

William woke up feeling one hell of a lot better. Strangely, he was still somewhat drunk, but he felt coherent enough to make it through the rest of the day. Glancing out the window, he felt that sliver of fear and doubt return as he saw, to his shock, that night had already fallen. *How long have I been out?* he wondered. The file was gone and so were the ashes. William wasn't upset that it had disappeared, figuring he'd either dumped the trash in a drunken stupor, or more likely, that it hadn't even been there in the first place.

The shrink said I might imagine things, he thought to himself. The shadow of the memorial plaque could be seen silhouetted against the window adjoining the hall, seeming to give off an eerie cast, almost as if it were glowing. The plaque, that horrible, ever-present reminder of the tragedy that had befallen the firm five long years ago, now seemed alight with life. William shook it off, as he had done with all the other strange things that happened that day. The appearance and then sudden departure of the file, seeming to fall from his mind as he thought of all the warnings they'd given him, all the sympathy for someone who had gone through what William had. *Survivors guilt, they called it,* he reflected.

Even though counselors had tried to tell William time and time again that the tragedy wasn't his fault, that he should consider himself fortunate, the words always seemed hollow, as if they were really telling him that he was the cause. Every sweet-tongued condolence seemed a condemnation telling him that he was the reason that almost every other member of his firm had been murdered, gunned down in cold blood. And their pity-filled stares were made even worse by the fact that deep down, William knew the truth. He tried to hide it, tried to tell himself that he was a winner, nothing more to it. William had been winning every case he had handled before the massacre, on a fast track to partnership, and at the time he wondered why should it be different, that he be one of the few to escape alive? After all, he was on a hot streak. It was only later that things had taken on their horrendous portent.

William stood up and faced the window overlooking the city lights below, a thin layer of fog marring an otherwise clear night. Tentatively, he ran his hands over the glass, feeling its smooth surface beneath his fingers, imagining the bullet holes, and the blood. The window had been replaced, the office scrubbed, the furniture new, and the carpet torn up to be redone with hard pine wood, but William could still imagine the holes, where the bullets had torn through. *I had a cubicle back then,* he thought, gazing out into the city of endless possibilities, wondering. The position of William's little workspace had been one of the only things that had saved him. The police had made that fact abundantly clear after finding a cowering William hiding in the women's room on the fifth floor. When the gunman had entered, mowing down everything in his path, he'd made the mistake of starting with the offices. *I wasn't a partner yet,* William thought, the sentiment filling him with a strange sense of emptiness, the hollowness of a hulled husk drained and ready to be thrown away.

William shook his head, trying to clear away the bad memories. Turning, he barely remembered to grab his briefcase before he was out the door, no longer wanting to be in that office, or the building in general. When he got to the hallway, he noticed that the secretary was gone. Glancing back, and hating himself for doing so, William was almost sure he could see the outline of a file on his desk.

✳ ✳ ✳

The subway station was deserted and William was beginning to feel an odd sense of déjà vu. He tried to tell himself it was normal, but wasn't at all convinced, wishing for some company in the underground transit station. Thoughts of his earlier encounter flashed through his mind, *the guy who knew my name,* and William was almost glad for the emptiness. Finally a few late night travelers meandered their way into the terminal, and although most of them looked as if they'd be taking bets on just how fast William could bleed to death if a problem arose, their presence was still somehow comforting. William thought back on the strange occurrences of the day and was especially bothered by the fact that he'd fallen asleep in his chair until way past midnight and no one had awakened him, almost as if he didn't exist. *Probably thought it was another drunken stupor,* he thought bitterly, but thought it an especially odd event because the office was locked up at eleven PM, becoming official policy after the tragedy.

The train was just pulling into the station when William saw the man. The lighting in the station was bad, but the face pressed grotesquely against the glass of the subway car behind him was unmistakable. The metro was slowing, the leering weathered grimace of the homeless man splitting into a grin as the train ground its way to a slow halt. *That's impossible,* William thought as he watched in terror as the man in the subway car behind him extended his tongue, licking the window in a manner that was greedily anticipatory. William willed his unresponsive extremities into motion, seeming riveted to the train, and in that split second of horror, he noticed something he had been too frightened to fully recognize at his first encounter with the crazed man. The face that leered at him, hatefully and longingly, the homeless man's face, was not that of a stranger. It was the same face he'd seen outside the window on the ride to the office, but deeper, more haggard and worn. It was the face from all his nightmares of the past five years.

William started to run, as the door to the subway opened, the familiar homeless man starting off the train at an unhurried pace. Terror's icy hands groped at William's flesh as he ran, knowing just where he had seen the man last. Five years ago, a crazed look of sadness in his eyes, the man had burst into William's law firm and started killing, taking the lives of every man and woman in the law firm he blamed for his pain… except one.

William didn't stop running, the entire time thinking, *Hillman's back…*

The streets were dark, and the bottle he'd picked up after making his way out of the subway hell was half empty. At every turn, William saw that leering familiar psycho coming back to finish the job. *What you are thinking is simply impossible,* he told himself. *It just isn't happening. The doctors told you this kind of thing could occur. What did they call it? Paranoid Psychotic Delusion Episode, or something like that.* And William certainly felt like he was well on his way there. He walked the streets and back alleys, out of breath and energy, trying to keep as far away from people as possible, fearing the sight of that familiar visage in a member of the crowd. *The man you thought you saw is dead. He's been dead for five years.* William shuddered at the thought. He had visited Hillman's grave, knowing as he did, that it was William, himself, who was responsible for the whole bloody ordeal.

Don't think like that, he admonished himself. It was the shrink's words filled his head, but it was sound advice. William tried to tell himself that there was no way he could have known what his actions would have led to, but there was a nagging part of him that could never let him fully accept that. He knew how he had acted, how far he'd gone to win a case. *And his wife... and his daughter...* William stifled these thoughts with two hearty swigs off the bottle, as he wandered down the street, heading in the direction of home. *I just can't handle it anymore. I'm finally cracking up.*

The darkness of the alleyway seemed to surround him, his footfalls resounding off cracked pavement. Trash lined every wall, rats scurrying around the piles of refuse for a late-night snack. A shadowy pile of rags and cans that could easily conceal a person lying in wait hugged the side of a trash bin overflowing with garbage, and William hurried his step. *I just don't want to see his face again,* he thought, realizing why the two faces he'd seen, the one in the window outside the subway car and the homeless man's, had seemed so different. The first one, the glance caught for a second in the window on the morning ride, was how Hillman had looked in court. *Before I destroyed his life,* William thought sullenly. The homeless man was how Hillman had looked when he'd massacred everyone he'd held a grudge for at the firm.

"You killed my father, and you made me lie!" William heard a voice, screaming at him from the side. In the darkness, William hadn't noticed her. She was leaning against one wall of the alley, a young girl about seven years old who looked oddly familiar.

William cut her off. "I never killed anyone, little girl." It was a stupid thing to say, but he was so shocked by her sudden appearance and accusations that he couldn't think of anything else.

Like everything about this night, this strange encounter reeked of something sinister, something uncanny. The girl's face… if he could only place it. His mind raced to make the connection. *If only it wasn't so dark,* he thought.

"What are you standin' there for? Are you afraid?! That's not like you at all." She took a step forward, "What's the matter, William, don't you remember?"

"No!" He screamed it, pushing the girl away. He realized who the girl was now and wanted nothing more to do with this growing nightmare. He had to get home, where it would be safe. Leaving the alleyway and the girl behind, almost expecting her to reach out and grab him like icy hands from beneath drowning water, he could still hear her shrill voice screaming behind him. Strangely, the voice seemed to follow William home.

*   *   *

William turned the two locks of his apartment
door with shivering fingers. *I'm home,* he thought, seeking relief, *nothing can hurt me now.* Fumbling, he rushed
over to the kitchen counter and the drawers beneath,
nearly slipping on the linoleum floor as he went. William
rifled through his kitchen utensils until he found what he
was looking for, a Colt .45 six-shooter that always made
him feel like a cowboy when he held it. He didn't feel any
of the usual sense of power now. Quickly snatching up
his quick-loader, six more rounds in a device made for
speedy reloading, he noticed just how the handle felt like
the chilly grasp of death. *I can't blow away the ghosts of
my past,* a part of his mind told him, but he refused to
listen.

Still panicked, William made his way to the
bathroom, stumbling. He needed some cold water and
medication. Fumbling the mirrored cabinet door open,
he withdrew the bottle of sedatives his shrink had pre-
scribed, and popped four of them, wanting nothing more
than to sleep. Turning the handle on the sink, he almost
expected blood to pour from the faucet, but the water
was clear and refreshing. William felt a cool sliver of relief, momentarily, only to be shattered as he glanced up to

see the mirrored cabinet door closing, of its own volition, suddenly whipping shut with violent force, as if it had been slammed. William watched as the mirror cracked and split asunder, sending shards flying everywhere. He felt the sting as the sharp glass cut into him, and could already feel the warm drip of blood on his face.

Almost as if on cue, William heard a familiar croon, causing him to once again pick up the pistol, "You weren't very nice to my daughter, you know." There was a sickening laugh to the voice and William placed it instantly. It was a voice he'd imagined incessantly over the past five years, the voice of Stacy Hillman. The woman, herself, had wanted nothing to do with William, who was so instrumental in winning her case, after she'd seen what the verdict had done to her husband and daughter, and yet, here she was.

"It was lies, all lies." William turned to her, the former Mrs. Lucas Hillman, now remarried and living somewhere in the Caribbean off the blood money he had won for her. And somehow she was here as well, a memory from his past, just as vibrant as William remembered, a slip of a dress barely concealing her pert figure, skin showing in all the right places. One hand held the gossamer fabric of her dress over her chest, the outline visible beneath, inviting, as it had been years before.

"Come on, William, you made me a lot of money. Us, a lot of money. Let's go for another round. I owe you." She dropped her hand and the dress fell, the athletic body still as he remembered it on all those late night house calls he'd made while prepping the case. "Come here, *partner*, you're definitely worth my time now."

At one time he had been turned on by her sultry allure, now he was repulsed, nearly sick to the point of vomiting. "No. No. I can't... all the guilt." William felt his hands beginning to shake. *This isn't real. None of this is real.* He tried to tell himself that, as Lucas' Hillman's ex-wife took a step closer, approaching, moaning with lust as she did, closing the space between them.

"No. You're not real. I'm imagining you. The doors were *locked*. They were locked, there's no way."

"Shhh..." She was in front of him now, one finger pressed against his lips, motioning for silence, while her other had grabbed for his crotch. "Just enjoy." William pushed her back with one fierce thrust, the naked woman flying back a few steps.

"Stay back." The lawyer raised his gun, the grip on which he hadn't loosened since picking it up, and pointed the barrel at her dead on. "You're not real. Stop haunting me. I couldn't have known how it would turn out."

"But it turned out that way and now we're both rich; we both have these great lives." She made a face that was supposed to evince seductiveness, but to William, it was as appealing as a rabid dog's snarling leer.

"Yeah, and Lucas Hillman is dead. Because of us. Because of me." William tried to take a step back, but was stuck against the bathroom counter with nowhere to go. "Now, I don't want to hear any more of this." He tried a different tact, fearing for his sanity. "I'm going to bed, and when I wake up you'll be gone."

Stacy licked her lips cloyingly and smiled, "I'll never be gone, honey-bunny. Never." She said the last with a grim finality.

Keeping the gun trained on her, as he'd seen in movies, doubting his shaky aim, William made his way around her, the heavy footfalls of his shoes on the tile floor sounding ominous in the scant space between them. "Don't come one step closer, or I swear, I'll kill you." She smiled as if to say 'you can't kill a ghost,' but said nothing. As he reached the hall to his bedroom she made her move, as if his retreat would somehow break the spell of her being there. Lunging, the naked woman was faster than William could have ever anticipated, and in that instant, he saw Stacy for what she truly was, her skin aglow, and her eyes fiery, ablaze. William fired, the bullets slamming into her body. William could see, sickeningly, her teeth barred like fangs. He fired again and again, until the faint clicking sound of the hammer falling on empty chambers was the only thing filling the silent aftermath, the body of Stacy Hillman, now a crumpled mess on the floor. A part of his mind was telling him that the cops would be there soon, but that didn't really seem to matter much right now, as shock filled every fiber of his being.

William's hands shook, and he took a tentative step forward, toward the limp naked form, now torn asunder by bullet spray. He had to get out. He didn't know exactly why, but something within him was telling him he had to run. William didn't even make it three steps before the body suddenly started to rise. Grotesquely, the bullet-riddled figure rose from the floor to face him. "You didn't think it would be that easy, did you?" Came the voice, though it was different now, deeper, more masculine. William took several backward steps out of the bathroom, hoping to make it out the door, but the *thing* cut off that avenue of escape. A few more steps had William in the living room, nearing the expansive window with the view he paid so much in rent for, the complete opposite direction from the door. The form before William's eyes began to shimmer and change, laughing the whole time in a cackling howl that only held chilling, blood-curdling rage.

William frantically tried to work the speed-loader, forcing the new bullets into the chambers, becoming caught up on the spent shell casings. But now facing him was none other than the same homeless man from the train, the vision of what had become of Lucas Hillman in his last days. "Do you like this look, William? Do you? This is how I appeared after you destroyed me. You obviously didn't like me when I showed you my wife. But you liked her enough *then*. Enough to ruin my life. Or perhaps you liked me better as my daughter, who you twisted against me with your lies." There was a sudden shift again and the figure that had only a moment ago been the homeless man, now morphed into the girl from the alleyway, the all-too-familiar face now easily placed. "No, this is better done in the body you knew me best." There was another metamorphosis and the figure before him became Lucas Hillman as William had known him best, as the courtroom defendant so many years ago. He was the shadow that William had dreamed about night after eerie night, the man who he'd driven to ruin, the face so often glimpsed in a mirror, or in a reflection out of the corner of his eye, the face he'd seen that very morning on the subway ride. It was his nightmare come to life.

"Well, after all these years, I finally have a chance to face my accuser. And don't get me wrong, it was *you* who was my accuser." Hillman was even wearing the same suit he'd worn in court, the one with wide lapels and faint pin-stripping, and he was enraged. "You twisted my wife and my daughter." Hillman took a step forward, a visible portrait of hate and vengeance. "We were having an amicable divorce until you took over. You had to make partner, William, didn't you? You had to do it at such a young age that you never cared who you stepped on. You slept with my wife during the proceedings. *My* wife. The papers weren't even signed yet and you twisted her, made her lie, just so you could for that big settlement. Just so you could be a partner at Meyer and Rose before anyone else."

William couldn't even say a word, his throat closed. The gun hung limply in his hand, unable to move, transfixed by his guilt, knowing that every word rang true. Hillman was before him now, and he pushed hard sending him back against the glass. "It was *you*. You who fed my Stacy lies. You who told her she'd make a better case if she framed me as an abusive spouse."

Lucas Hillman looked William dead on in the eye when he spoke. "I swear to you, with God as my witness, I never so much as laid a hand on her. It didn't work out, but I still loved my wife, William. You took that from me. When she finally meets me here, you know what, I'll forgive *her*. Because I can forgive her, but it's *you* I can never forgive. You're the one who turned my daughter against me. It was you who made my daughter, *my own daughter*, make up stories that I molested her. She was still young enough to believe your lies, especially when you had Stacy telling her it was true. That was how you imagined her, and the judge bought every damn word you said. Every word you put in her mouth. You bled my company, William, you destroyed my life. You took everything I had. I hunted you down that day, you and everyone who had a hand in that case, and, you know what? I failed. But I won't fail this time, William. I will have my revenge."

William opened his mouth to speak, but Lucas Hillman's fist slammed it shut, smashing into his jaw. Hillman didn't stop, striking out with years of pent up rage, blood flying across the window. William grabbed for his gun, but Hillman knocked it from his reach. William dove after it, adrenaline giving him a burst of strength and speed. He felt the cold steel in his hand, knowing he would have to aim for a head shot. Hillman grabbed the lawyer excruciatingly by the hair and lifted William to face him.

William pushed savagely, knocking Hillman back a step, against the window, and didn't hesitate, pushing the gun against the Hillman's mouth and pulling the trigger. The report of the blast was loud and Hillman released his grip, even as the bullet continued on, shattering the large window behind him, shards of glass and blood flying everywhere. Hillman seemed dazed, and William continued the assault, firing the remaining five bullets into Hillman's body. The ghost from the past staggered backward with each shot, swaying, near the edge of the shattered window, hovering on the brink, one foot from the precipice and the abyss of night beyond. William pulled the trigger again. Empty. Seeing Hillman teetering, William seized the opportunity, rushing forward, seeking to push the wavering form through the window. It was only too late, in a headlong rush, his momentum carrying him forward, that William noticed Hillman was smiling. William passed right through the ethereal form of Lucas Hillman, and into the cold night beyond.

✳ ✳ ✳

Lucas Hillman watched with satisfaction as William Jacobs connected with the impassive pavement of the streets below, the lawyer making a surprisingly quiet thud, blood seeping and soaking the concrete. The form watched for a moment longer, shimming and turning aglow with radiant light as it hovered in the apartment before slowly fading away, Hillman's words lingering long after, "You should've known it was a ploy William. I learned from you. You should've realized that you can't kill a ghost."

*   *   *

"So suicide, huh?" The man said with a smirk.

"Yeah. That bastard had everything and look at him now."

"Well, money doesn't buy happiness right?" At this, both the workers had a good laugh. "Hey finish up this thing okay? I'm getting hungry." The man was almost done with his engraving, his partner watching to make sure it was done right.

"Another one dead in the New York streets. Not much of a headline."

The man shrugged at his partner, surveying his work. "Yeah, but what *is* nowadays?" The engraver stood, satisfied, and turned to his co-worker and nodded. They both headed to the elevator, smiling at the secretary on the way out, who returned the grin, not at all seeming the least bit sad. As the pair made their way out the office of Meyer and Rose they looked back at their work one last time, satisfied, the memorial plaque bearing one more name, "William Jacobs". Applicants were already lining up for the vacant office.

Hooked

He could feel them digging into his skin, the sharp jagged barbs tearing through the muscle and the tendons. Every fiber of his being cried out in agony, his voice wracked with pain. When he'd first awakened in this living hell, suspended from some strange unknown ceiling by hundreds of fishhooks and tackle, Benny had screamed and thrashed, only to find that any movement dug the rusty metal hooks deeper into his flesh. He wanted to close his eyes, but the sharp hooks that had been threaded through his eyelids cut him when he did. "What did I do to deserve this?" he muttered through a mouthful of blood, "Why?" There were jagged barbs through his lips, making comprehensible speech nearly impossible, and Benny could watch the trickle of crimson fall to the floor like raindrops or tears, adding to the growing pool of sanguine quickly accumulating beneath him. Benny was naked, the multitude of barbs ripping into every exposed surface, keeping him lifted at least four feet off of the floor.

The room was bathed in shadow, and try as he might to recall how he had found himself in such a terrifying position, Benny found he couldn't remember. He could picture himself going to bed the night before, blissful sleep taking hold. He could vaguely envision the cold hand covering his mouth, but after that there was only darkness, no recollection of how he got there or any explanation of why he wasn't roused by the painful insertion of hundreds of rusty fishhooks into his flesh. Nothing could be drawn from the well of blankness. Even the extreme excruciating agony of being hoisted aloft was a non-existent memory, the first recollection coming into focus only after he had awoken suspended, thrashing in a world of pain. That he had been kept unaware the entire time suggested drugs, yet, for the life of him, Benny couldn't figure out why. Questions of where he was and what he was doing there, in this world of macabre torture, ran through his mind. Suddenly, a sharp screeching, like the sound of an old door being drawn open, split the stillness of the room and Benny closed his eyes, wincing as ragged gashes cut into his eyes, stifling a scream as he tried to pretend he was still unconscious.

The room seemed to grow alive with light, blindingly bright, and Benny fought to keep his eyes closed. *Not yet, you've got to think of how to get out of this,* he thought to himself. "It's no use," a voice said and Benny found that it seemed uncannily familiar, the words almost a condemning response to his optimistic thoughts of escape. "I know you're awake, Benny. I've been watching you. Studying you. Watching you suffer."

Benny heard a noise and immediately a burning unparalleled pain racked his body as his eyelids were wrenched open involuntarily and the sharp corroded hooks dug into his irises. His vision blurry from the eye wounds, Benny could see a hooded figure, eerily reminiscent of an executioner, yanking down on a set of fishing line, obviously attached through pulleys to his eyelids. Benny's frantic thrashing caused by the pain only made the other hooks in his body dig deeper.

"You like my handiwork, Benny? I know you like *your* handiwork," the masked figure said, approaching.

"I… I don't know… what… you're talking… about," Benny sputtered, seeing a healthy smattering of blood soaking the floor below.

"Oh, I think you do, Benny. I think you know quite well. I think you even recognize my voice." The masked figured paused for a second, almost in reverie. "And I thought I had the perfect set up. A nice little town. No problems. Ha," the voice laughed, though there was no humor in the tone. "It's the ultimate irony."

Benny shook his head inadvertently, before realizing what he was doing and the hooks tethered to his neck dug through his skin, some ripping free and taking flesh with them.

"They called you 'The Fisherman' because of the way you lured them in," The masked figure continued. "It was your MO. Tell the little girls you'd take them on a fishing trip. Only none of them ever returned. You don't know how long it took me to track you down, Benny. The Green River guy was at large for over twenty years. I got you in less than five. You kept moving, but I tracked you down. I read every news snippit, every little article in the paper, looking for a foiled kidnapping attempt, a dead body discovered. You liked to use fishing line to tie them up while you raped them." The masked figure was within striking distance now and he lashed out, grabbing Benny's arms and yanking down, the hooks tearing through his flesh, drawing a hail of blood. "How do you like your fishing line now, Benny? The police couldn't find you, but I did. I never gave up. Not after what you did to my daughter. After that, I could never forget you. And now I'm going to use all my *talent* to torture you."

Benny opened his mouth to scream but the masked figure was already removing his hood. Realization struck as Benny saw the face unveiled. It was a face he'd seen wracked with agony at the little girl's funeral, a face he'd seen day in and day out for years. Now there was only marked terror at seeing that familiar visage. "You were my neighbor for five years and I never even suspected. I was trying to live the good life. And you had to take my daughter, Benny. My only daughter. In my day, I killed more people than you ever could fathom. You see, Benny, I was a murderer too. But I found religion and I changed. Moved to suburbs and started a family, but then you came into the picture. Can you imagine that? Two serial killers, living side by side. Only I'm trying to better myself. But you brought me back, Benny, for a 'one night only' show. I thought about things long and hard after you took my daughter from me. I thought that maybe if I hadn't been who I had been, if I hadn't done what I had done… but then I thought that if I hadn't then I wouldn't be able to stop you and do what I'm going to do to you. But the philosophy lesson is over, Benny, now it's time for some schooling in pain. And believe me, I'm an excellent teacher. You're going to suffer like I've had to suffer. You see, for you, the agony is just beginning…"

A Dose of His Own Medicine

Dan's hands trembled uncontrollably as he searched for his pills. They hadn't even shaken this badly when he'd killed his first victim. His heart raced, terrified he was going to die. *All this because I couldn't sleep,* he told himself. That was why he'd seen the psychiatrist, why he'd taken the pills, on his shrink's orders, all because he had insomnia.

Now, he felt ill. He'd tried to cough up the medicine, but all he could manage was a few dry heaves. His intestines seized and clutched like a cold fist in his gut. *If only that smug psychiatrist were here now,* he'd have some advice, Dan thought frantically, recalling his delight at the doctor's look of disgust when he'd heard the reasons for the sleepless nights, conveyed with bloody detail. Dan was smart, well aware of doctor/patient privilege, knowing his shrink was helpless to stop him.

Head throbbing, his vision blurred as he finally found the medication bottle.

Squinting to read the label, realization suddenly set in. He staggered forward, reaching for the phone, falling after only two steps. Crashing to the floor, darkness encircling him, Dan thought of his psychiatrist, the bottle of pills rolling towards him, almost mockingly, the prescription boldly asserting: *One pill daily. WARNING: DO NOT EXCEED DOSAGE- SEVERE INJURY OR DEATH MAY RESULT.* As Dan made his final connection, he thought, *the shrink had said, "take at least three."* He realized that perhaps the psychiatrist hadn't been so helpless after all.

The Taxidermist

From the second he'd laid eyes upon him, Carl had thought that there was something strange about the taxidermist. And that was before he'd found the severed finger. The proprietor of *The Stuff of Legends Taxidermy* was a short bulbous wreck of a man, an ogre-like figure who sported a fiery red 80's mullet and several days of unshaven stubble. His markedly unkempt appearance made the taxidermist seem deformed, the man's stomach bloated beyond belief. The taxidermist had abnormally plump fingers, surprising given his trade, and Carl couldn't help but feel an instant repulsion. When Carl entered the shop with his prize hunted buck in tow, he had almost turned around and left when he saw the man behind the counter. A strange sense of unease had filled him at the sight, but after driving miles with a dead deer in the bed of his truck there was no way Carl was going to turn back just because of some simple misgivings.

"When do you, uh, need it by?" The taxidermist asked. Carl noticed the hesitancy in his voice.

"Phil, right?" Carl inquired, glancing at the name tag and trying to appear genial, although he just wanted to be away from the odd little man. "Look, this is a prize kill here. I need it ASAP."

"Well, there are other people I've been attending to…"

Carl stood a head taller and outweighed the taxidermist by at least forty pounds and he was getting ticked. "You know, I really couldn't care less about them. It's not every day you bag a stag like this. This has gotta go by my fireplace. This is a showoff piece, not some lousy tourist fish."

The little man behind the counter did not seem in the least bit frightened by Carl's tone. "I'm sorry, but like I said, I have other things I'm working on and I really can't…"

Carl's earlier disquiet was now dulled now by anger, and the hunter in him took to the fore. "Look. I don't like you and I really don't care what you have going on. You're the only taxidermist in this town and I didn't come up here all the way to hunt just to have to drag my kill back home. It'll be ruined. So, why don't you just get on it for me? Okay?" He leaned over the counter and seized the man's collar in his meaty palms.

For a faint instant it seemed as if the little bald man was going to lash out violently, a mad look in his eye, but then it was gone, replaced by mild acquiescence. "Whatever you say. The customer's always right."

With these simple words, the taxidermist effortlessly extricated himself from the Carl's grasp in a move that surprised the large hunter. The taxidermist then walked over to the slain stag and hefted the huge buck over his shoulder, all the while seeming to exert no strain. It was a feat that made Carl a little jealous, still aching from the strain it had caused him when he had brought the buck in.

Carcass in hand, the taxidermist was nearly in the back room when Carl raised his voice to speak. "Hey, Phil, how..."

The man made no response, either not hearing or not caring, as he disappeared through the door.

Perturbed at the strange sequence of events but satisfied with the way things had turned out, Carl found a promising looking wooden chair and reclined in it, waiting for the taxidermist to get back an estimate on time and price. If Carl had not gotten up to grab a hunting magazine off the taxidermist's counter, he probably wouldn't have noticed the finger. It was sitting in plain view, as if it were something as innocuous as a discarded cigarette butt, like a discarded trinket to be given no more thought, but until that moment the hunter hadn't even noticed it. Now, Carl nearly screamed, turning a ghastly pallor. There was no doubt it was a human finger, dried blood congealed just below the second knuckle.

Carl knew instantly something was very, very wrong and his hunter instincts took over. Withdrawing his large, ever-present fixed blade, Carl wished he had a gun handy. The thought of running for help crossed his mind, but Carl was a tough guy. He wanted answers and that was what he was going to get, even if they came from a taxidermist skewered on the end of his knife. Silently, cautiously, Carl crept toward the back room, a strange sense of exhilaration filling him, as thoughts ran through his head that he was doing what he loved best: hunting. Only this time the prey was human.

As he made his way back, Carl found the room empty, the taxidermist nowhere to be seen. He couldn't help but feel the eeriness when he saw the absurd emptiness of the room. No animals adorned the shelves, no trophies were tagged and ready to be collected. There were only a few small decomposing animal corpses lying on a stainless steel workbench, but they appeared neglected, as if they had not received care in a long time. Strange machines cluttered the room and although Carl had never set foot in a taxidermist's workshop before, they seemed a bit elaborate, excessive, considering the obvious lack of business.

Carl took one slow step followed by another as he desperately tried to stay silent. The room seemed deserted, and his hunter's instincts put him on edge. Several parts of the workspace were bathed deep in shadows thrown by the various pieces of machinery, giving the odd little man ample places to hide.

Slowly, Carl made a circuit of the room, constantly on guard. The eerie lighting, florescent illumination coming unknown sources, caused the hunter to jump at things that weren't there.

At one point he screamed, "Aha!" thrusting his knife into a pool of shadow only to hear the resounding clamor of a utensil tray as it clattered harshly to the floor. The ominous reverberation seemed like a cacophonous roar to the hunter's ears. Carl shivered, feeling like he was hunting ghosts.

Taking more hesitant steps into the darkness, Carl spied the outline of a door. It appeared to be an entrance to some kind of storage room or freezer, and Carl grinned a little, his fear seeming to melt away as a thick coat of adrenaline enveloped his body. The hunt was back on. Carl was so intent on the new room that he failed to hear the cabinet beneath a workroom sink slowly open.

Carl pulled back the storage room door handle and peered inside. The space was dark, darker than the previous room, and Carl fumbled for a light switch. When he found it, the faint illumination of a single hanging bulb flickered momentarily. Carl nearly dropped his knife in shock, when he saw what filled the storage space.

The room was packed, and it seemed to Carl as if he had somehow stumbled upon a repository from the Twilight Zone. Icy tendrils of fear clutched his stomach, the bile rising in the back of his throat as he took in the scene. They looked like statues covered with cloth, but their shapes were undeniable and there was little doubt as to what they could be. But Carl knew he had to be sure. He had to know that it was not his overactive imagination playing tricks on him. Hesitantly, Carl reached forward, his hand shaking, and thoughts filling his head that he should have gone for help.

Nothing he could have envisioned in the dark recesses of his mind could have prepared him for what he saw when he pulled back the tarps. His knees went weak as his assumptions solidified into fact. What stood before him was a human being, a stuffed trophy of human flesh. The complexion of the dead man was waxy and the embroidery on the employee shirt said "Phil". Two pinholes showed where a name tag had been removed, and it didn't take a genius to figure out that this was the true taxidermist.

Carl had only a split second to think as he heard a laugh behind him. He was so startled he lost his balance, falling backward and dragging several of the stuffed dead bodies down on top of him. They clattered to the ground and Carl found himself immersed in stiff flesh, desperately trying to extricate himself.

"So, now you know my secret." The odd little man stood silhouetted in the doorway, a broad smile creasing his face. Rage boiled inside Carl as he dug his way out of the bodies, pushing aside corpse after corpse. Fear filled him as he noted each body he pushed aside seemed to be that of a hunter.

As if reading his unvoiced thoughts the strange taxidermist impersonator answered, "You have your prizes. I have mine. You call yourself a hunter. I'm the *true* hunter. And now you can be a part of my collection." With that the light in the room died as the door swung shut with a resounding finality, the last thing Carl hearing was the faint turn of the lock sliding into place.

A Haunting Proposal

"Help..." came the raspy croak of a woman's voice, throat parched from screaming, as she raced down the weed-encrusted path, running as if her life depended on it. In the distance stood the object of her fear: a macabre house, ominous in appearance, its weatherworn siding fallen into disrepair, its paint peeling and worn, standing in stark relief against a starless sky. Her wail echoed in the still night air, but no one would heed her cries, "They're trying to kill me!"

Adam and Carrie laughed at the terrified woman, as she tore past them in hysterics. Adam eyed his girlfriend with a sinister gaze, and chortled, "You're next honey!" He made stabbing motions with his hands, reminiscent of Hitchcock's *Psycho*, "This year your birthday present's to die for." He oozed with ghoulish charm. "This haunted house is supposed to be the most spectacular in the state and I've arranged for something extra special just for you."

Carrie was curious about his words, but merely smiled and nodded pleasantly, getting lost in the ambiance of the place. The attention to detail was remarkable. Realistic looking skeletons crawled from open graves in the yard, the eaves cluttered with flocks of restive bats. Granite tombstones and cobwebs sprinkled the yard with their distinctive flavor, and a rusted weathervane creaked ominously on. The owners seemed to have spared no expense at creating The Ultimate Haunted House and Carrie could see how it lived up to its apropos title.

Adam said something else but Carrie, immured in her surroundings, didn't catch it. This place was truly beyond compare. Carrie voiced her thoughts. "I can't believe how real this place looks. It's so great having a boyfriend who indulges me like you do." The seductiveness in her tone was music to her beau's ears.

Adam gave her a peck on the cheek. "If my Halloween-born honey wants a scare, then a scare she'll get."

"I'm shivering already." It was said in jest, but Carrie softened the blow by wrapping her arms around her man, hugging him close.

"We have the house to ourselves for an hour. Don't do all your shivering now. The best is yet to come." There was something foreboding in his voice that didn't quite settle well, but Carrie was too enraptured with her surroundings to give it a second thought.

Carrie could only gawk like a child opening her first Christmas present. It had been a long-running quest for Adam to try to frighten Carrie, and he had never truly succeeded entirely. Carrie had a bit of an obsession with fright. In the three years they had been dating, the couple had seen nearly every horror movie ever filmed, had escaped death's clutches on a wide variety of dangerous extreme sports, and experienced their mutual favorite pastime: an annual Halloween pilgrimage on Carrie's birthday touring different haunted houses around the country. But tonight was different from all the others. Adam had something else in mind.

A worm-eaten wooden chair sat empty on the veranda, rocking of its own volition, a forbidding greeting as the pair approached. Shingles dangled precariously from their perches, threatening to give way at a moment's notice, a nice touch adding to the bewitching atmosphere. The creepy mansion seemed perfect in every detail.

The splintered wooden steps even creaked with protest as Carrie and Adam approached the entrance, and the sound could almost be mistaken for human voices, eerie moaning supplicants begging for release. The front door was ornately carved, a montage of the morbid and the gruesome. Adam grasped a grotesque looking gargoyle door-knocker and proceeded to rap loudly. Measured footsteps could be heard in the distance heeding the call. The door crept open slightly, a hunched figure holding it ajar, whispering to himself in a tongue that was foreign to the couple's ears, almost otherworldly. Recognizing guests, the creature, whose back was humped in camel-like fashion, his clothes sagging appropriately, actually smiled. It only made him appear more sinister, his smile revealing jagged, yellow teeth that were crusted and broken, set into gum work that was black as the night sky.

The fiend screeched in a voice that was horrific to the senses, a craggy squawk that was tantamount to the grating sound of nails drawn across a chalk board. *"Welcome my friends. Welcome to your death!"*

Carrie giggled as atmospheric mist drifted from the inside the house. The creature seemed genuinely shocked by her response, apparently unaccustomed to such cavalier sentiments. Adam nodded as if to say, *Yeah well you don't know Carrie.* Stepping carefully inside, the couple found themselves in an expansive dining hall lit solely by several rusty, tarnished candelabras. The centerpiece of the room was a massive mahogany table covered with a moth-eaten tablecloth having lost all semblance of its former shape. A darkened chandelier hung from the ceiling, its glass cracked and dirty. "Wow, this is even better than the one you took me to last year!" Carrie crooned.

"Just wait..." Adam answered fiendishly, "this place is different, there's so much more."

They entered a dimly lit library, their hunched guide wordlessly leading them along, Carrie gazing about in wonder. Her eyes took in the unusual sculptures of bone, one seemingly made of human skulls in varying shapes and sizes, stacked upon one another in a maze of burning candles. Bookshelves lined the room, holding an impressive collection of occult and witchcraft lore. Adam jumped as the silence was broken by one of the larger tomes as it fell to the stark marble floor.

"A little jumpy, huh?" Carrie laughed playfully as she bent down to retrieve the book. She chuckled even louder as she read the title: *Evil Made Easy*. Catching a glint of silver flickering in the candle glow, she strained to get a better look in the scant light. Upon closer inspection, she realized what it really was, a butcher knife, lying in a pool of blood. Touching the blade, she was surprised to find just how real the blood felt, warm and oozy, not like the fake stuff used in typical haunted houses. And the blade was sharp, too, almost too sharp. Not the usual rubber knife trick. As she examined this new discovery, enjoying every moment of her adventure, a harsh tap on the shoulder shook her from her thoughts. "Oh Adam", she chucked though with considerably less mirth, "this is…"

Carrie's vocal chords froze in mid-sentence as she realized that both Adam and the hunchback were gone. In their place stood a hideous creature, clad in dark, blood-stained robes, his skin deathly pale, a living cadaver. His nails were gnarled and twisted and seemed to fold upon themselves covetously. Carrie smiled slightly, her initial shock passed, and whispered, "Nice touch." The creature returned her smile, revealing razor-sharp incisors etched with the same, almost too real kind of blood. "Adam… come on out," Carrie cried, "you've got to see this guy," but there was no reply. Adam had never left her alone in a haunted house before, and for the first time since arriving, she began to feel a slight tinge of concern.

Abruptly, the creature cackled, pulling a very deadly looking knife from the folds of his robes. "Don't bother calling for your precious Adam. He can't hear you. But don't worry sweetheart, you'll be joining him very soon."

As the knife slashed towards her, Carrie felt the blade come dangerously close. "Are you crazy?!" she screamed. "This isn't funny any more. Adam, come on out!"

"He's dead," the creature repeated as he swung the knife again. Carrie raced from the room, tripping in the darkness. Haunted house employees weren't allowed to attack visitors. Or so she had always been led to believe.

But this place is different. She heard Adam's words resound in her own head. Carrie could feel the creature gaining on her with every step, seeming to feel his fetid breath on the nape of her neck. Terrified, she ran, not knowing where she was going but just knowing somehow she had to get away. Her mind reeled. *Where's Adam? Oh God, what's going on?* At every turn Carrie looked frantically around for her love, trying to blot the creature's words from her head: *he's dead, he's dead, he's dead...*

Carrie's frantic flight led her through the immense mansion, taking corners heedlessly, only trying to find Adam and escape this true house of horrors. Her hurried steps brought her to an eerie laboratory replete with blood-stained operating tables and dozens of specimen jars filled with vile-looking substances. As she rounded another corner, she came upon an operating table larger than the rest, a Frankensteinish creature tethered to it, struggling against its restraints. Carrie let out a scream that was deafening, but she didn't slacken her pace. The table barely behind her, Carrie could hear the sound of the straps tearing as the monster leapt from the table and joined the chase.

Now, two creatures in pursuit, Carrie could feel her heart pounding faster and faster until she thought it might burst. Her muscles ached and her legs nearly buckled as she stumbled into a brightly lit hall. The room was an eclectic collection of devices of torture: iron maidens and racks, thumbnail screws and whips of various design, the walls lined with coffins. Immediately, her gaze fell upon the newest looking of all the wooden caskets, the only one not weathered and rotted with age. It was not just the box itself that captured her attention, but more so, the intricate engraving upon it in large gothic script: **Adam.**

Carrie screamed, "No... no... Adam!" Her world seemed to collapse. How had things gone so wrong? Tears rolled down her cheeks and if the monsters had seized her that instant it was doubtful she would have even noticed.

Her gaze fixed solely on the box. She *had* to see, she just *had* to. This couldn't be her Adam. Her Adam was alive, he had to be. Carrie flung the lid open. Tears stung her eyes as she recoiled in horror from the sight of her beloved Adam lying prostrate, a knife protruding from a gaping chest wound, blood still oozing from the gash.

In the midst of hysteria, Carrie grasped frantically at herself, her muscles coiling and uncoiling, telling herself that it wasn't true, it couldn't be true. It was simply impossible. She shivered as the unreality washed over her, carrying her farther away like a tidal wave until suddenly a very dead Adam sat straight up, effortlessly pulling the bloody knife from his chest. "Come closer, Carrie, I've been waiting for you." Carrie took a few cautious steps forward, seeming to float in space and time. She watched in strained anticipation as Adam slowly reached into his breast pocket, the dream-like nature of it all cascading over her like a waterfall. Her anxiety and fear turned to fascination as Adam pulled out a heart-shaped box and thrust it toward her. "Will you marry me?" he asked with a huge grin. That was the *surprise*. That was what was *special*. A proposal, and just the way she would have always wanted it to be.

Before she could answer, a tremor shook her body, Carrie frantically clutching her chest falling to the ground in pain. Adam screamed, leaping from the coffin, "I think she's having a heart attack!" The color drained from his face as he knelt at Carrie's side. Just then, all the other coffins in the room burst open and out rushed Carrie and Adam's friends and relatives from their ghoulish hiding places, their faces solemn with fright and concern. In the ensuing pandemonium as friends and monsters alike filled the room, no one seemed to notice the thin smile that slowly crept upon Carrie's face, until she softly answered, "Yes, I will." With a wry grin, Carrie sat up and smiled. "Gotcha! I couldn't let you have all the fun."

Adam jumped up, shouting, "She all right, and she said yes!"

The crowd breathed a collective sigh of relief and then proceeded to go wild, screaming, "Congratulations!"

Adam pulled Carrie aside and held her close, whispering, "That wasn't funny. I was really scared."

"Yeah, wasn't it great?!" she laughed.

Adam and Carrie embraced each other as the creature in the tattered robes and the Frankensteinish monster worked the room, pouring champagne for all the ecstatic guests. The hunchback returned with a plate of finger food appetizers. Adam removed the beautiful diamond and ruby jack-o'lantern ring from the heart-shaped box and slipped in on Carrie's finger, while a haunting happiness filled the room.

A Matter of Perspective

Mark knew he should have been enjoying himself. The bright lights, the scents and sounds of the New Orleans festivities greeting him at every turn. All the candy a fourteen-year-old could stomach, and the overwhelming air of enjoyment filling the night. But, despite it all, Mark Underhill couldn't shake a feeling of impending disaster. He had tried to tell himself it was just the masks, the All Hollow's Eve costumes and the way they twisted and leered, but he wasn't convinced. Deep in the recesses of his mind, as much as he tried to deny it, Mark knew what he has seen. It had been the *thing,* the physical manifestation of the *thing,* he was sure of it. As much as he would have liked to believe it was just some incredible coincidence, some reveler's outfit resembling the witch's artifact or some trick of his imagination, Mark knew better. What he had seen had looked too much like the voodoo doll for it to be anything but the wicked embodiment of arcane magic.

All Hollow's Eve had never been Mark's favorite holiday, but tonight had turned from a mediocre time on the town to a complete and utter nightmare. But, as much as Mark desperately wanted to go home, desperately wanted to call it a night, he just couldn't. Doing that would prove that his mother was right, that he was still too young to be out with no curfew. Mark shuddered despite the warmth of the evening, knowing with the prideful certainty of an adolescent that he had to see things through to the end, no matter what.

A bump at his shoulder made him jump, and Mark turned in a flash, certain that the *thing* had found him. His eyes wide with fear, Mark found himself greeted only by the sight of an inebriated elf walking with an unsteady gait, who kept himself from falling only by the aid of his prop long bow. Mark tried to laugh it off, chiding himself for being so on edge. He was supposed to be enjoying himself. It was a holiday. But Mark assumed that anyone who'd seen what he had seen would feel the same way.

The evening had started off on such a good note. A sweet sugar rush from too much candy filling him, and a beautiful young woman in a cat outfit giving him a smile. The feline-attired femme had looked at least a few years older than Mark, but it was obvious from the seductive cat calls she made that she was interested. Mark had approached her with a bolster in his step, feeling big and wanting to impress, and that was when the night had taken its first wrong turn. Crossing the cobblestone of the French Quarter, Mark plowed headlong into a very authentically-attired witch, the woman's ancient appearance seemingly not attributable to make-up, her gnarled cane looking as if it came from another world.

Normally such a polite young man, it shocked even Mark when he heard the words coming out of his mouth, his normally polite 'excuse me' becoming a rude, 'out of my way lady'. He had wanted to show that he was tough, that he was cool. The elderly witch had leered at Mark, appearing as if she'd just been struck physically. Politely, almost regally, in a manner from a forgotten time, the woman admonished Mark to mind his manners, fixing him with a cataract stare. At the time Mark had laughed, uttering a dismissive, "Whatever," as he turned to look for the feline-costumed girl of his dreams. That was when things had gotten weird, the sorceress stranger saying nothing more as she reached out and pressed a tiny object into Mark's hand. With that, she seemed to disappear into the night, a faint smile cresting her lips, a knowing smile.

For a second, Mark just watched her go, his hands clasping the object, completely baffled by the strange turn of events. Pushing the bizarre encounter from his mind, Mark had tried to once again find the young girl in cat attire only to realize that she, too, was gone.

Uttering a curse, Mark had set his sights to the prospect of other girls and more candy, only remembering, almost as an afterthought, the object the witch had imparted upon him. He glanced down with frustration, but when he saw what he held in his hand, an instant shudder of revulsion and fear surged through his body. It appeared transparent, translucent to the point of insubstantiality, and Mark knew what he was seeing. Living in New Orleans his whole life, Mark had encountered voodoo dolls before, but never one like this. There was a texture to the doll, but to the naked eye it appeared as if there was nothing in his hand whatsoever. It was only when the light caught it at certain angles that there even appeared to be anything there at all, a shimmer the only telltale sign of its existence.

Turning his hand to drop the object, Mark felt an icy stab of pain as he realized the doll wouldn't come free, the tiny object seeming to cling to his flesh, almost becoming a part of it. Mark shook harder and finally the witch's doll fell to the ground. In the grip of panic, Mark didn't even look back as he set off for another section of town, a sudden and overwhelming need to be as far away from the strange encounter and all it portended filling him as he headed off into the night.

* * *

An hour later, with a bellyful of candy nestled safely in his stomach, Mark had been starting to feel okay again, thoughts of the strange woman and the doll having faded to an almost distant memory. He was leaning against a store window, watching the humorous belligerents who'd had more than a few too many and taking in the flavor of the city, when he first saw the *thing*. At first, it had seemed to be just a shimmer in the crowd, a strange trick of lighting, but as the phenomena of illumination continued, Mark realized that there was definitely something happening in the street. And with a sinking feeling, Mark realized just how much the strange shimmering sensation reminded him of the voodoo doll, only on a much larger scale. It seemed as if the texture and the fabric of the street was taking human form, the strange translucent *thing* heading in Mark's direction. Mark dropped his candy, thinking of the strange witch and her gift, and the horrible similarities. *This can't be happening,* he thought; but despite his mind's attempt to rationalize, the apparition kept coming closer, becoming more and more tangible with each step. The very air itself seemed to congeal into substance, a creature, which was fast approaching.

Run, his mind had told him, and Mark listened, taking off down the street, ducking and dodging through crowds in a city he knew like the back of his hand. When the throngs of people grew too thick, alleyways presented new avenues of escape, as Mark rode the waves of people through street after street trying to elude whatever it was that was following close behind. Every so often, Mark would think that he had lost his pursuer, only to see a translucent glint or glimmer under a street light. Now, Mark was at a loss. He knew he couldn't go home. Not only would that prove that his mother was right, but it also would lead the *thing* right to his door step. No, Mark knew that option was out, and so was calling the police. As much as he desperately wanted to, especially as fatigue began to wear him down and the ache in his legs became more than just a minor pain, Mark knew he couldn't really *tell* anyone because, quite frankly, who would believe him? Mark wasn't even sure if he believed himself. People would think he was drunk, or worse, insane.

After taking a few sharp corners, Mark leaned up against a wall, bathing himself in shadows as he momentarily tried to calm his ragged breathing. Several minutes passed with no signs of a shimmer. Mark, however, didn't want to press his luck, and as soon as he got his wind, lost himself in a crowd, the whole time trying to stay relaxed. A few minutes passed, a time of constant searching, in which Mark saw nothing. Not a single glimmer or shimmer to disturb the night. Minutes ticked by and the young man was almost beginning to convince himself that he had imagined the whole thing, jumping at things that weren't there. That was when Mark saw it again, faint, still far off, but approaching nonetheless, and with a speed that was frightening. *It's so quick,* Mark thought, but he didn't have time to contemplate it at all as he once again took off running.

Glancing behind as he fled, Mark wondered if the *thing* would even be able to grab him if it got close enough, the apparition seeming to be made of nothing more than air and light. But thoughts of the substantiality of the voodoo doll made Mark sure that if the *thing* got its hands on him, he was done for.

People seemed to fill the night in a swirl of colors and masks, and Mark felt stifled by them as he made his way through the crowd. A green devil laughed groggily, groping at an overly-tall mermaid leaning against a wall. A ruddy dwarf lay prostrate in the street forcing people to go around, over, or on top of him. Tweedle Dee and Tweedle Dum locked arm-and-arm heaved dryly onto the concrete. It was a mass of confusion and Mark capitalized upon it. Picking up the pace, he wended his way through the crowd. His head throbbed as exhaustion tugged at him, everything seeming to blend into a kaleidoscopic montage as he went. A man on stilts, blended with a man covered coated head to toe with paint, in Mark's mind. A black vampire coalesced with a soccer player, and the whole world seemed to be swirling in a blender.

To Mark, it appeared as if he were watching the whole thing from afar, his body not really his, as fatigue tore away at him. The tired adolescent could hear someone screaming for 'candy', a person or food, Mark didn't know. The lighting of the streets grew dimmer, and, as Mark trudged on, he knew that he was slowly wending his way off the main thoroughfare, though there seemed to be little he could do about it, backward glances telling him that the *thing* was close, very close. Mark ducked down one alley and then another, and veered into another still.

A half-conscious bum called out to him, "What's a matter boy, seen a ghost?" Mark could hear the laughter trailing after him as he continued on. He kept running, his legs positively burning as he went. "Hey kid watch it!" He heard a terse voice saying, and it took Mark a minute to realize that he'd run headlong into someone.

Mark didn't hesitate, "Listen, you've gotta help me. There's this *thing* after me. Some crazy lady sent it, and oh, I'm so sorry… I just want her to know I'm sorry… I didn't mean it… I was trying to be a big man… and I…" His words ran together, coming out between winded breaths, tears welling in his eyes.

Mark was silenced by the same voice as before, the tone gruff and implacable. "Look kid, everything's gonna be just fine okay, now just listen to me, all right?" Mark smiled, looking up at the man. There was confidence in the stranger's posture and Mark knew that this was someone who could help, someone who could stand up to the *thing*.

Mark tried to calm himself. He had reached the end of the line and he was exhausted. He almost couldn't believe it. Things were going to be okay, the man had said. Mark was going to get help. The stranger ran his tongue over a gilded incisor as he spoke, tugging at the twill of his coat. "Look, kid, everything's going to be okay now." The man reached out a meaty palm and tenderly ran his hands over the young man's shoulders. Mark looked behind him and saw that horrible, familiar shimmer at the end of the alleyway. He knew, the *thing* had found him.

Time seemed to blur, happening with an incredible speed. In one second, Mark was whipped around and slammed up against the wall by his would-be hero. He felt the man's body pressed up against his, the smell of sweat and day-old gin assailing his senses. "Everything's gonna be just fine, kid. Just do exactly what I tell you." Mark was being smothered, constricted by this man's presence.

Mark was incredibly confused by the change in the man's demeanor but, still felt safe. This was a man in control. "Now listen, you do exactly what I say. We've gotta make this quick." Relief surged through Mark, knowing that this was a man of action. "If you're lucky kid, and you do everything I tell you, maybe I won't kill you when its over. Give me all your money, right now…" It was only after a moment that Mark realized the full import of the words.

"I'm not messing around kid, now, I said…" A faint shimmer grew around the horrible betrayer's neck, and Mark heard his next words choked off with a faint gurgle. Suddenly, Mark was free of the pressure but still found himself trapped between the robber and the shimmering *thing*. Mark tried to move but found every escape attempt blocked by the struggle, the man who had tried to rob him finally ceasing his frantic writhing and falling to the ground in a heap. Mark shivered, feeling as if he had just hopped out of the frying pan and into the fire, backing up against the wall as far as he could, alone with the *thing*. And now Mark knew what it was capable of.

Mark closed his eyes, not wanting to see what would come next, wishing desperately that he could just see his mom and be held by her one more time. Mark prayed fervently and sincerely beneath his breath. He knew if he were able to someway escape that his life would change. He wouldn't argue so much, he would help every old woman across the street, anything, if he could just see another day. Mark's imminent death brought a moment of clarity as he realized that all the possibilities for good, all the possibilities to help wouldn't be always be there. It was something most people didn't think about, especially when they were young and had their whole lives ahead of them, but Mark thought about it. And, as time progressed and he didn't feel pressure around his neck, Mark Underhill hesitantly opened his eyes.

Mark found himself alone, wonderfully, wonderfully alone in the alleyway, the sounds of merriment far in the distance sounding nothing so much like cries of joy and promises of second chances and possibilities. Perhaps, Mark wondered, that was what tonight had really been all about, what the woman had been trying to instill in him, the knowledge that he always had a choice and sometimes a single act could affect so many other things. Honestly, Mark didn't know, but he did know that he owed an apology to his mother and a big thank you prayer, and those were things he would be happy to deliver. With a broad smile on his face that seemed to shimmer in the moonlight, Mark started home.

Angel of Mine

"Why does he hit me so much?" Sandy asked her unseen friend, tears welling in her eyes. She didn't expect a response. There had never been anything except for silence in reply to her agonizing pleas and unanswered questions, but somehow today the silence seemed all the more ominous. She didn't know if it was just her imagination, but her unseen companion seemed to be exuding more anger than normal in the wake of the beating. To Sandy it seemed as if her friend was fit to be tied, the feeling of anger as palpable as a humid mid-summer swelter. Drying her eyes, Sandy winced as she touched the purplish-blue bruises forming below both eyes. Seeing the red indentations where her wrists had been held, she wished as she had so many times before that her friend would just say something. At least that way she would know she wasn't crazy. She didn't think she was, and at her young age she had no compunction about acknowledging her otherworldly companion, a figure that was more of an intangible feeling than an actual visible being, but for some reason she felt that it would be nice to be certain.

Since Sandy had discovered that she was not alone when her stepfather hit her, the beatings had been more tolerable, but that just made her wonder if some part of her mind was imagining the whole thing to lessen the pain. She still remembered the first day she had felt the presence, a strange sense of warmth enveloping her as she caught a glimpse of what looked like a faint shimmer behind the raised meaty fist before it fell into her stomach, almost as if the unseen force was trying to stop it from coming down.

Sandy had been filled with a glimmer of hope, but that was quickly extinguished as she felt the first blow. After that, Sandy realized that her companion, like her, could not stop the destructive force of her stepdad. The beatings hurt, but knowing they were coming from a man who was supposed to be caring for her was far worse. Sandy just wished her real father was still alive, knowing he would never have allowed this to happen. But he was gone and the abuse persisted, terrible, demoralizing and heartbreaking.

Still, Sandy had never given up hope, finding resolve in knowing that she was not alone. Nursing her wounds today, though, she felt close to sinking into the pit of despair. The exceptionally harsh round of fist blows and belt lashings had been excruciatingly painful, her memory stained with visions of her stepfather's bloodshot and hate-filled eyes boring into her, his body swaying, loaded down with so much alcohol it seemed he might topple over. Only he never did, and the hurt still reigned down. Sobbing into her tiny hands, Sandy could almost feel her unseen companion's white hot rage. And in that moment, something changed. Sandy could not say what exactly, but it was almost as if her companion's anger was infusing her with strength, giving her a resolve she didn't know she possessed. Tired of the tears, Sandy sat up on the bed.

The movement hurt, her arm aching inside a cast as an unhealed fracture sent a shiver of pain up the bone, but she was not deterred. The break had been a present from her stepdad, one that had spurred a surprise visit from child social services on the account of her treating doctor's suspicions. But her stepdad was far too clever, had been doing this for far too long, and he'd purposely laid off until the government officers had come and gone, satisfied that Sandy was in good hands. Only the threats of what he would do to her mother, graphic and disturbing in their detail, and made worse still by the fact Sandy knew he would carry out his word, kept her silent. When child social services had left, the beatings had doubled, making up for lost time, and tonight was worse than most.

Feeling the rage sink into her belly, one fantasy after another ran through her head: knives slicing skin, a gunshot's booming echo, a pyre to burn away the sins of her stepfather. After a long moment they faded, ashes on the wind, and then the tears came, Sandy realizing that fantasies were all they were, intangible, as unattainable as taking flight. Exhausted, more physically drained than she could have possibly imagined, Sandy laid back down on the bed, pressing her face in the pillow. When sleep finally came it was mercifully dreamless, belying the tears dried on her cheeks and the bruises, reminders of the horror she'd endured. The respite didn't last long, Sandy sitting bolt upright as she heard her door creak open. Her heart dropped and her stomach churned, knowing without even having to look that her stepfather was back.

"Well, look at 'chu," her stepfather slurred. "Layin' there all spread out like a whore. Well, maybe that's just what you are." His voice thick with drink, spittle flecking his lips, Sandy knew exactly what he wanted. Her body shaking, Sandy turned, reaching for her pillow, as if it in someway could be a magic talisman, warding the evil away. Closing her eyes tight, the tears blurred her vision.

Despite all the pain her stepdad had inflicted, never before had he said anything like that. "Yer mom doesn't want none of this, but I know you do," he said, resting one hand on his crotch as he stood in the doorway, struggling to maintain his balance.

Sandy couldn't even bear to watch, her room a living nightmare. Her mom had always sheltered her from the worst, taking the beatings or the things done behind closed doors when he was uncontrollably drunk, but now here he was, like a monster from the abyss, horrifying in his brutal reality. Despite the fear she felt for herself, Sandy prayed his mother was okay, knowing she'd never allow this if she was conscious or able. Hearing creaking footsteps, Sandy mustered the courage to peer beyond the pillow, seeing the dim outline of stepfather, his hands struggling furiously with his belt as he staggered toward the bed. Despite the horror of the moment, a panicked part of Sandy couldn't help but wonder where her unseen companion had gone, the presence she'd always taken comfort in knowing was there suddenly gone, vanished. Sandy trembled, realizing the awful truth. She was horribly, horribly alone.

Suddenly the bed felt ponderously heavy as her stepfather's massive weight sank down on it and Sandy scrambled back against the headboard. His pants were down now, a pointed bulge in his stained briefs a herald of the horror to come. The tears flowed freely down Sandy's face, wondering why she'd been deserted, left alone to this terrible fate. Sandy glanced up at the ceiling light hanging above her bed that she had once, in what seemed like another life, asked her real father if it was the light of God, and silently prayed. The desk lamp beside her bed began to flicker as she felt the massive hands of her stepfather gripping her tiny legs in their meaty grasp, spreading them apart as he struggled to get closer.

Sandy could feel his ponderous bulk atop her now, sweat-soaked skin pressing against her as he fumbled with his crotch. She could smell the pungent whisky odor, the sickening scent of his flesh as the booze dripped from each pore, all of it making her want to vomit, bile rising in her throat. Then everything seemed to happen at once and the world turned upside down. In one instant she was helpless, a victim, and in the next she felt a sudden rush and the return of her unseen friend. Her companion seemed absolutely alight with rage, the anger a palpable force infusing her with a strength she didn't know she possessed.

A part of her mind told her that this simply couldn't be happening, that she was dreaming, delusional. Breathing hard and deep, Sandy stopped letting reason guide her and relied on instinct, taking the plunge. She was too young to know anything about the paranormal, or the power of spirits, but she was young enough to believe and accept the truth of it and that belief gave her the power she needed to push her stepfather momentarily off of her. Then the repetitive flicker of the lamp beside her bed caught her eye, and Sandy didn't hesitate, grabbing the blunt object and smashing her stepfather across the head with it. The blow wasn't enough to down the large, drunk aggressor, but it sent him reeling, knocking him back toward the center of the bed and allowing Sandy to spring from his grasp.

Sandy was running to the door when it happened, the light above the bed suddenly bursting apart with otherworldly force, jagged shards of glass flying everywhere, driving into Sandy's stepfather's exposed flesh, tearing into his head and his eyes, ripping holes in his neck as the explosive force drove the glass. Blood soaked the bed, but Sandy didn't notice it, running headlong out of the door and straight into a pair of grasping hands. Screaming, wondering if somehow her sick stepfather had brought a friend along for the fun, it took her a minute to realize she was in the embrace of her mother who had bruises to match her daughter. Then Sandy was crying and her mother was too, whispering gently in her ear, "Never again, never again," as they stoically watched the lifeblood drain from the monster on the bed's numerous wounds, seeing him struggle for air that would not come through a torn throat.

It would be years before Sandy came to understand what had happened in rational terms, how spirits were believed operate on different frequencies and have the power to affect electricity, but at that moment she understood the truth intuitively, knowing that her prayers had been heard and her father had come back for her. He had not forgotten about her. Not now, not ever.

Double Jeopardy

He waited with bated breath as the twelve filed back in. He knew what their presence meant: verdict. The trial had gone on for what seemed like ages and Peter James' stomach churned. His lawyer was the best money could buy and had put on a flawless defense, but in Peter's mind there was always a sliver of doubt, even though no body had ever been found. Peter knew he hadn't killed the guy, as much as he'd wanted to, but the circumstantial evidence was strong. His daughter had been beaten to death by her abusive husband and Peter's comments after new broke of the husband's disappearance did him no favors. As the weeks progressed, Peter's diatribe of fire and brimstone, virulent exultations that the husband was burning in hell, only served to add nails to the slowly building coffin of suspicion. When the police raided Peter's mansion and found a trace of blood in the kitchen, charges were filed. Peter had told the police candidly that the husband, his son-in-law, had cut his finger on a chipped glass months earlier, but that didn't stop the indictment.

Now it was the moment of truth and Peter took one deep breath after another. His stomach churned, his hands clammy. *Some justice this would be,* he thought bitterly, *Justine is rotting in the ground and I'd be rotting in prison for a crime I didn't commit, though God as my witness I wish I had.* His breath came so sharply it sounded like a bull's snort, the exhalations seeming a counterpoint to the footfalls of the bailiff walking over to give the jury verdict back to the foreperson for announcement. And then, in an instant it was over, the words read: Not Guilty. The pronouncement resonated in Peter's head and nothing could have sounded as sweet. In the whirlwind that followed, the handshakes and hugs from friends, and the sneers and jeers from the husband's family, the only thing that Peter could do was smile. He'd been vindicated.

*　　＊　　＊　　＊*

Night had fallen and the mansion seemed empty and dead. *It will never have life again now that Justine's gone,* Peter though bitterly, a tear rolling down his leathery cheek. A glass of one of the world's most expensive cognacs, Louis XIII, was in hand, the vintage perfectly balanced and flavored, but even three glasses four fingers deep had not dulled the pain. His eyes stayed riveted to a picture of his daughter, her smile the only one in the expansive estate. "I wish I would have done something sooner," he whispered, his voice a harsh croak, hoping his daughter could hear him, "If only I'd known." Shaking his head, his body trembling, Peter called for his butler.

"Yes sir," a tall, rigid man with gray hair said stoically.

"I'm ready," Peter said, draining the glass.

"Very good sir," was the only reply.

Peter inhaled deeply, praying for courage. When the butler returned he was not alone, dragging a man tied hand and foot with ropes along with him. The festooned captive shook, trembling violently and Peter, almost dismissively, noticed the gag. "Remove it," he said slowly, everything seeming dream-like. He'd envisioned this moment for so long and now it was here. The bound man was naked, his body pale, muscles that once might have been toned now atrophied. Peter only watched as his butler did as bidden.

"No… no… no… why…" came the broken pleading once the gag was removed, the captive man falling to his knees.

"Please," Peter said, rising from his chair. "Don't take me for a fool. Both you and I know why you're here."

"But... but..."

"I have to wonder," Peter said, turning his back to the man, "did it make you feel powerful?" One hand, steady now, reached out and opened his desk drawer. A large window that gave a gracious view of the city skyline provided a glimmer of moonlight to reflect off the implements contained on a velvet lining.

"I didn't... I... I..." the man whimpered.

"Both you and I know you did, so there's no use in denying it now." Peter exhaled deeply. "I just want to know I'm going to make you experience what it means to feel powerless, I'm going to put you in Justine's position."

"Why..." It was a statement not a question.

"I know you're not asking why I'm doing this, we both know that, so I'm thinking you're wondering why I waited so long, why I let them try me."

The pale corpse-like former man nodded through tears and for a second Peter wondered if he should even give him an answer. In the end he made his decision. "I wanted them to," Peter said. "I wanted the cops to find blood and that's why I planted it. You see there's something called double jeopardy in our legal system. They were waiting too long to charge me so I had to speed up the process. It was a win-win. They didn't have evidence except for the little bit I provided. It was enough to charge but not enough for a conviction." Peter smiled. "I even had a backup plan. If they somehow convicted me I could dump you, alive and well, and my conviction would be dismissed." For the first time in a long time, Peter laughed. "And now, when they find your mangled corpse, if they ever do, they will never even think of charging me. You know why? Because I've already been acquitted of your murder, a murder that's about to happen. I probably don't even need to use gloves for what I'm going to do." A small smile split Peter's face as he pulled on a glove, "But I'm never one to take chances." Slowly Peter reached down into the velvet-lined drawer, withdrawing a silver surgical tool, the glint off the blade looking so much like a glimmer of hope, even as the corpse-like pillar of flesh pleaded for mercy that would never come.

Charity

"I'll always love you," were the last words Edna spoke, her lips pale, nearly translucent as her face relaxed. She sunk into death happy, content that her money would help so many and that her legacy would live on, belying the blood flecked on her lips from lungs worn raw by pneumonia. Edna's eyes flickered in their sunken sockets one final time and then she was gone.

Hal smiled at her words, inwardly laughing, remarking at just how naive she could be. There would be no charity, Edna leaving him as the sole beneficiary had seen to that. Hal would be the sole inheritor of millions. *She really believed I'd give her money to her charities,* he mused, pleased with the thought, *but then again the old hag actually believed I cared about her too.* Hal was careful not to let so much as a glimmer of his delight show, his countenance a mask of sympathetic pain, just in case she hadn't quite passed over yet. Staring at the sad faces of the gathered family and friends, Hal could barely contain the joy he felt, knowing that all in attendance would be left with nothing from the estate. Maintaining the charade, one he had kept up for what seemed an interminably long time, Hal leaned over and kissed his betrothed in the manner of a grieving widow. Edna had been twice his age, though he had wined her and dined her as if she were the most beautiful woman in the world, and after the things he had done, things that made him cringe just thinking of them, Hal figured one more kiss was a small pittance for all he stood to inherit. "I'll cherish you forever," he said as he gave the dead woman gave one last embrace.

Seeing all the loving faces surrounding the hospital bed, those same faces sneaking furtive glances of disdain in his direction when they thought he wasn't looking, Hal couldn't help but chuckle inside knowing that he was going to have the last laugh. Silently the doctor in attendance nodded and closed Edna's eyes. Hal smiled inwardly, knowing that soon he would be a very, very rich man indeed.

The girl batted her lashed and everything about her exuded sexuality. Full pouty lips and hair that was as gold as the morning sun complimented huge breasts and an outfit that just spelled 'Heartbreaker'. She wasn't the take home to mother kind, but the type that would fulfill every twisted desire, and right now that was just what Hal was looking for.

"Hey there," she said, seeming to notice his stare, and though the words were mouthed from across the bar but their intention was clear to Hal.

The girl tossed her hair lightly back over one shoulder in a manner that was clearly sensual and lit up a cigarette. Images of what he would like to put between her lips instead of an ash stick filled Hal's mind and he wondered absently if the girl was a hooker. Not like it mattered now. Probate had closed, and despite the protests of jilted charities, Hal was a man with money in the bank. *After all that wrinkled flesh,* Hal thought, *I need something something tight and young.* The very thought brought a smile to his face and warmth to his loins.

Hal smiled back at her over a beer, making no attempt to hide the fact that he was staring at her chest. The fact that she didn't blanch or turn away seemed like a good sign and getting up, Hal sauntered over to his drop dead gorgeous admirer. "Hey sweet thing," were the first words out of his mouth, oozing unchecked desire. Hal didn't care if he sounded cheesy, he was of the mind that when a person had money, those things ceased to matter.

The girl seemed to buy into it, replying with an interested, "You're looking good." Her tone was overtly sexual and the naughty things alluded to in her tone made Hal once again think she was prostitute. Strangely, that seemed to turn him on more, knowing that the small talk would be kept to a minimum and it would be straight to business.

If only all women were this easy, Hal thought with a smile. "So are you, honey. Come to think of it," he said, picturing himself suave as he produced a cigarette from his pocket and setting it aflame with a gold Zippo, "I'd say you light up this whole place."

"Oh really?" she asked playfully, putting one hand on the flesh of her exposed chest to emphasize her cleavage.

Hardly able to keep his desire in check, Hal made his intentions clear. "Hey, you want to get out of this place?"

The girl nodded, and Hal felt the tremor of excitement rise within him. "Come on then, we're going to my place." Hal smiled, thinking of how impressed she'd be with his extravagant mansion.

With a demure smile, the woman said, "That's just what I had in mind."

*   *   *

"Was it as good as you remembered?" came the voice from the darkness.

Hal lay back with a contented smile, their furious lovemaking a memory that would always be imprinted on his mind, at least, he reasoned, until his next great conquest. She had insisted on darkness but that was okay because now he felt as if he could just sink back in it. Hal was a bit confused, still wondering if the girl was a hooker because she had asked for nothing in return, heading straight to the bedroom as soon as they'd made it through the door, but he figured it didn't really matter. He'd gotten what he wanted, and he thought to himself that was the way it was going to be in the future. *Taking what I want,* he thought with joy.

Still immersed in that blissful notion, Hal squirmed beneath closed eyelids as the distinctive glow of a light being turned on invaded his sanctuary of relaxation. "Yes," he said, "All right yes, it was good. Come on, turn the light down and come to bed."

For a second there was no reply but then Hal heard a faint chuckle, one that held no warmth. "No Hal. That's not what I asked. I asked if it was as good as you remembered."

Unsettled, but refusing to let the weirdness kill his sense of bliss, Hal asked lackadaisically what she meant as he turned over languidly to see what was going on. Hal got his answer as he opened his eyes, finding himself face-to-leering-face with his worst nightmare. There was no denying it, even as his frantic mind screamed that it was impossible. Edna was back. There was no way it could be and yet somehow here she was, long buried but now back nonetheless, skin putrid and rotted, wrinkled beyond description. "I had to come back Hal," the Edna, her eyes penetrating into his own. "I trusted you with my money and you deprived those who really need it."

Hal recoiled, wanting to scream but having no voice, as Edna pointed one gnarled accusatory finger at him. As she began to approach, all thought left him and he felt his tenuous hold on sanity slipping. "Oh, come on, honey, don't think I've forgotten," her ominous and somehow *earthen* voice bellowed. "Today is our anniversary and I figured I had to come back to this body and pay you a visit and set a few things right."

Edna reached out with the tattered hand that was more skeleton than flesh, fingers caked with dried blood and broken nails from digging her way out of her grave. Her touch was ice, chilling Hal to the core and again he tried to scream but could not. Slowly, with great purpose, Edna's hand climbed up his bare chest. Hal's skin recoiled at the touch, pocking with gooseflesh, as the impossibly cold fingers almost burned his flesh.

"You should have paid more attention when you were with me, Hal. How I appeared in the bar is how I looked when I was young. I must have showed you pictures a hundred times," she chucked, a laugh that sounded like her death rattle. "Come on Hal, didn't you miss me?" Then her hand was on his throat and she was atop him, mounting him with skeletal flesh. "Sure you do," she said with a smile. "You miss my kiss..." With that she leaned in, pressing her bloodless lips to his. The last thing Hal heard, a whisper as he was held in her embrace, was the admonition, "And now it's time to give..."

✳ ✳ ✳

The detectives were perplexed when they found him. "I just still don't get it," the first, a rookie without much time one the force, said.

The second, older and seeming far more jaded, shrugged absently. "Who knows with these rich people? They're all a little batty if you ask me."

"Yeah, I guess you're right. Still, it's creepy to write your last testament in your own blood before asphyxiating yourself. But, who are we to deny his last wish right?"

"Yeah," the older detective said, jotting notes down on his pad as he stared one last time at the strange scene they'd come upon: Hal's lifeless body on the bed and scrawled in his own blood a single word above the headboard. "If that's what he wants then that's where all his money will be going. I'll try to contact his lawyer to draw up the papers."

The younger detective just nodded, still shocked by the whole thing. A plastic bag tied around the head with an electrical cord was an unusual way to commit suicide and something about it didn't set well with him. But, with no signs of a struggle, the rookie knew his superior officer had pretty much shut the book on the matter. The money was going to go to a good cause, he reasoned, and in the end sometimes that was all that mattered. Glancing back up at the dried blood and the word it spelled one last time, the young detective couldn't help but shake his head in puzzlement as he said softly, "Charity."

Field of Ghosts

She shivered despite the muggy warmth, and Isabella couldn't remember a time in her short life when she had been so scared. Not just scared but petrified. The only time that came close was just six months ago, back when her father was still alive, and she had made her first break for the fences. Everyone in the compound knew it meant death to try to escape, worse sacrilege as they were indoctrinated to believe their place as slaves was their due, but her and her father had not cared and they had been *so close*. Then the tragedy had struck, the whip crack of misfortune piercing deep and hard. Just as Isabella was about to make it over the compound fence, into her mother's arms and the freedom the outside world provided, away from the grasp of the Loving Arms Commune, her dad had been savagely struck down by a Child of Peace, the proctors of the community. Isabella had plummeted to earth, her body falling like her hopes, and the last memory she had of her father was of him mouthing the words, "I'm sorry princess," as the blood frothed on his lips and the sadistic guards drove their spears deeper. After that all she remembered was pain, the pain of loss and the physical pain of the beatings for attempting defying the Loving Arms' tenants of faith, foremost among them never ever leaving.

Running now, alert to each noise, every small motion in the fields, Isabella's fear eclipsed even that of that horrible day. She glanced back over her shoulder, praying the Children of Peace were still far behind. Isabella could hear the bark of their dogs, vicious hounds which scoured the outskirts of the compound near the fence to prevent escape, and knew they couldn't be that far off. Isabella prayed, as she had prayed every night for another chance to escape. Thinking back on her second chance at freedom it seemed like a miracle in and of itself. During the first attempt, her mother was the only one who made it out to safety, and Isabella had resigned herself into thinking she'd never again get the chance to escape let alone see her mom again. And then one of the boys who would occasionally be allowed to go to the nearest town for the few items the commune could not make, a boy whose obvious desire for Isabella overcame his indoctrination, had told her that a woman was asking about her. A few cryptic messages were exchanged, carefully, so as not to draw attention.

Isabella found out little about what had befallen her mother after the escape attempt, but a plan was hatched, her mother promising to meet her at the place of their last escape and to bring some new friends for help. Finally, after what seemed like an eternity, Isabella had once again been given the 'privilege' of working the Loving Arms fields and she hadn't hesitated in setting up a plan to make a break for the fence. Now, Isabella knew that there was nothing left to do but hope, and pray.

Fighting her way through brambles, the foliage became denser with each step, the vegetation thickening into a virtual forest as she reached the outskirts of the massive compound. Isabella battled tremors in her legs as fatigue tugged at them, only adrenaline and fear spurring her forward. She could hear the baying sound of the dogs behind her, and she knew that the Children of Peace would not be far behind. Isabella couldn't help but cringe, certain that they were gaining. As she ventured another backward glance, she could see nothing but foliage. Then, turning back, as she forced her aching and burning legs into motion, she saw the tree. Bramble bearing bushes had obscured it from vision until the last moment and in that split-second, try as she might, she knew she was going to fast to avoid it. An instant later, Isabella crashed headlong into the tree. Her vision blurred as she saw stars and Isabella just prayed nothing was broken. Dazed and disorientated, Isabella forced herself forward, knowing she had to move.

Isabella's head swam with pain as she ran, stumbling through a world that seemed horribly out of focus. Then she was on the ground, her foot caught in a depression, the sudden change of elevation sending her sprawling. Tears welled in her eyes as Isabella clutched her aching shin. Struggling to get up, Isabella watched in disbelief and horror as her knee buckled and she fell back to the ground. Drained and petrified, Isabella found her leg unable to support her, and the tears came harder. She could hear the sound of barking now almost upon her and Isabella knew that the Children of Peace had to be close.

"Mommy," Isabella cried, struggling to get to her feet, tears stinging her eyes.

Hearing the baying cry of a dog coming from the right, Isabella forced herself into action. Using a will she didn't know she possessed, Isabella pressed forward, taking one pained step after another, still dazed from her impact. Another bark, followed in suit by others, heightened to a crescendo of hungry calls and Isabella ran blindly, branches striking her in the face as she hurried on. From the corner of her eyes she could make out blurry shapes tromping through the brambles and she knew that the dogs were flanking her, not quite able to catch her but trying to cut her off. The fence was just ahead, but to Isabella it seemed a world away.

Abruptly the foliage died off, giving way to a solid stretch of dirt before the chain link and horrid images burst into Isabella's head, envisioning her father's agonizing death as she ran. The terrifying thoughts, coupled with the dogs, their salivating jaws chomping and now almost upon her, nearly made her give up, lay down and beg for mercy, but what she saw on the other side of the fence gave her strength. Her mother was there, just as Isabella knew she would be, waiting for her. And she was not alone, standing with three large men all in blue, bearing huge smiles on their faces. Isabella's heart soared as she realized that was the help her mother had brought. Her heart bursting with hope, Isabella needed no encouragement to hasten her pace, but her mother and the strangers were shouting anyway, urging her on.

Out of the corner of her eyes, Isabella could see the frothing maws of four attack dogs, two on either side, closing the distance as they honed in, quarrying her, trying to corral her. On the open ground they had no trouble making up the distance, and Isabella could feel the pain in her legs building to an almost unbearable heat. Risking a backward glance, she saw the first of the Children of Peace, their red jumpsuits looking like bloody heralds of doom, emerging from the bramble.

"God, please help me," she prayed and then she was at the fence, her hands on it, grasping at it as her eyes blurred with tears. She didn't know how she'd found the handholds, or the strength to climb, but once she had a grip, Isabella was up in a flash, beginning to scale the fence, knowing her life depended on it. Isabella was halfway up when she felt the teeth digging into her leg. The sharp pain of the bite set every nerve ending alight with agony. Shaking the dog's fierce jaws free with a power she didn't even know she could possess, Isabella was momentarily able to move only to feel another dog tearing at her, ripping her shoe off, and biting into her Achilles tendon at in the process.

The pain was excruciating, all sensation to her foot seeming to flee in that instant, and without the support of her foot Isabella nearly tumbled into the hungry mouths of the dogs. Engulfed in a web of fear and hurt, she almost gave up, almost released her grasp and sank into the teeth of oblivion, but the sight of her mother gave her strength. Grasping one handhold and then another Isabella forced her way up the fence, being careful not to put much weight on her injured foot. Her pace slowed and she watched with horror as the first of the Children of Peace began to climb the fence. The realization forced her to move faster, and seeing the massive floodlights at the top, Isabella knew she was close.

Catapulting herself onward, Isabella strained to reach, the stretch making her feel as if her arm would pull free from its socket. And then she had it, her hand gripping the post supporting the light. The grip was easy and she hefted herself over the rise, feeling the strong hands of the strangers helping ease her descent. And then Isabella was safe, wrapped tightly in her mother's arms, crying with joy and relief. "I knew you'd be here," Isabella said gratefully, comforted by the warmth that only a mother's love can provide. The strangers her mom had brought along stood guard, the same beatific wild smiles on their faces. On the other side of the fence, Isabella could make out the departing figures of the Children of Peace, their heads hung low as they sank back in defeat.

Comforted by the knowledge that she was safe, her mother whispering the whole time how she had never given up hope, Isabella still felt the need to ask about her new protectors. "Mom, who're these guys who helped me?"

"Oh, Isabella, you just wouldn't believe. These people are so wonderful, so unlike the Loving Arms. They're a group of people who just want to protect others." A faint flicker of unease crept into Isabella she looked around, seeing the people her mother had brought, her supposed saviors for the first time. That was when the dread began, seeing glazed eyes, eyes that mirrored her mother's own. "And they have this great leader," her mother continued on, "a guy who really helps. He has a place, a place where we can be safe, a place where we can live with our new family." Seeing the mindless nodding of the strangers her mother had brought, Isabella felt the tremor of terror creeping over her. And as her mother began to lead her away, prodded by the smiles and nods of her new family, Isabella felt the tremor of dread magnifying into a tidal wave, seeing the fence she had scaled and envisioning the one likely to come.

Glancing up at the fence, she saw the spot where her father had died, so near the floodlight that she had used to help her over, her eyes tearing up. *How?* she asked herself, her dad, and God, wondering, after all she had been through, how this could be happening. She didn't know if it was just the frantic delusions of her panicked mind, but she swore she could see her father sitting atop the fence, a smile on his face. He was translucent, ethereal, but in some way real, and while the rational part of her mind told her she had to be imagining it, a part of her knew that it was really the spirit of her father.

He looked younger than she remembered, powerful and strong, but she knew even if what she was seeing was real, and she hadn't gone crazy, it would do her little good to save her from the insanity all around her. "Daddy," she pleaded, and her father's spirit seemed to hear, because the ghostly form turned to her, a look of pleading in his eyes. Isabella's mother seemed to hear as well because she followed her daughter's eye line.

Isabella's breath caught in her throat as she saw her mother's stare. The crazed look softened, and in that instant she knew that her mother was seeing her father too and something was being passed between them. And then something miraculous happened. Isabella watched as the life flooded back into her mother's eyes, the glazed look gone. Suddenly she clutched at her chest, almost dropping to the ground. "Oh Ben," came the words, "What have I done…"

The burly strangers, alerted that something was going on, looked up at the fence as well. Seeing the sudden change in Isabella's mother, one of the larger ones grabbed her arms. "You've lost your way," he said, "we need to take you to the leader." Still, the strangers' eyes searched the fence, wondering what had caused the sudden change in their Isabella's mother.

As they did, Isabella's mom leaned down, whispering to her daughter, her words now clear. "Your dad says look away."

Isabella didn't understand but she obeyed, and a second later the world seemed to be on fire. The floodlights, powerful as they were, could not have generated the bright force they currently were exuding, the force of ten thousand suns seeming contained in their glare. Intuitively, Isabella knew it was the work of her father and as she heard the screams of the burly strangers, blinded by the otherworldly light, she knew her father had saved them. Seeing the would-be-saviors turned captors clutching their eyes, Isabella grabbed her mother's hand. "I'm so sorry," she started but Isabella silenced her, prodding her to action. The two of them ran, the roads blurring as they took one after another, trying to put as much distance between themselves and the commune and the strangers as possible. Only after they were far away did they finally slow, acknowledging that were not being followed.

"I'm so glad you're back," Isabella's mother said, wrapping her daughter into her arms, the true embrace that Isabella had been awaiting for so long.

For a second Isabella said nothing, thinking she would keep careful watch on her mother to make sure you never strayed into another cult again. Still, she figured after what passed between her father's spirit and her mother, she likely didn't have much to worry about. Pushing those thoughts aside, knowing that they were safe, she said only, "I'm glad you're back too. I'm glad you're back too."

A Brief Case of Horror

Liam let his thoughts drift as the subway car sped on, trying to relax. He'd seen the way the panhandler had looked at him when he'd gotten on, and it still ticked him off. He tried to push the dirty look he'd gotten for snubbing the guy from his mind but found it difficult. It was getting late, and he was more than tired. The noon meeting at the firm had run into lunch, making it a vending machine meal once again, and the early evening meeting had turned into a late night debacle. There were problems, big problems, with one of Liam's cases, and everyone had vowed to stay until things were handled. *Yeah, like that happened,* he thought bitterly. By the end of the meeting the partners were no closer to reaching a decision than they had been at the beginning, and with mutual irritation, they had decided to call it a night.

Dreamy thoughts of a missed four-course meal at the Ritz Carlton ran through Liam's head as he stared at the ceiling, grimly wishing the advertisements lining the subway train could actually dole out food instead of just teasing with it. A disembodied voice informed him of the approach of the next terminal. Fragments of his irksome case repeated in Liam's head like a broken alarm clock just out of arm's reach. The problematic case in question was a simple possession rap, ordinarily a cut and dry deal where all the defense had to do was pocket their retainer, file a few worthless motions and then just plead it off to the judge's mercy; a kid caught with two ounces of heroin who said that the drugs weren't his. To Liam, it really didn't matter whether the drugs were his or not, guilt and innocence were just matters of how a lawyer could spin it. And in the law's eyes, possession was tantamount to guilt.

Liam opened his eyes and studied the other subway patrons, scoffing as he did. It was always a game with him, to see just what dregs the public transit system could drag out of the woodwork, and who he had the ill luck to be stuck with. He'd thought about a car, but New York was a subway city. And the voyeuristic allure of surreptitiously studying people was too great a thrill to pass up. There was a girl on the train tonight, all of fourteen, wearing more make up than Madonna and sporting less clothing. *That's another one destined to become a welfare mother,* Liam thought with disdain. *Glad to see my tax dollars will be hard at work bringing up her love child.* A man in a commando suit with a wooden appendage sat uncomfortably on the hard seats, his good leg tucked beneath the prosthesis. *What war did you fight in buddy? The battle of who gets the last 40 ouncer? Late night brings 'em out, that's for sure.*

The last occupant in the car, sitting at the far end, looked the most normal of the bunch. *At least he's got a coat and briefcase. Maybe he actually works for living.* The man in question could have been the dictionary definition of 'an average Joe'. He wore a trench coat that looked a few seasons too old and tad bit too warm for the weather, but Liam shrugged, *whatever floats your boat.* The man's thick lapels were pulled high, and the hat he wore did wonders to obscure his face. If Liam was a paranoid man, and had not lived in New York his entire life, he would have found that a little strange. As it was, the inhabitants of the Big Apple seemed to have been the inspiration for the old saying, 'it takes all kinds'. With no more interesting passengers to gawk at, Liam once again turned his thoughts to his troubling case.

The law was pretty clear on the subject: possession was nine-tenths of guilty, but Liam had happened upon one of those one-in-a-million cases with a loophole large enough to drive a truck through. Liam smiled, thinking that the true beauty of it was he could milk the kid for a hefty fee and, in the end, he'd still come out looking like a saint for getting the case dropped. The problem though, wasn't the case, it was the kid. He'd run out of money, and as Liam Shooter was fond of saying, "lawyers win cases, they don't open charities." And that left the question of what to do about the kid. Liam, as a senior partner, had come to one very firm conclusion: no money equaled no acquittal. That was the way the system worked.

"Hey, buddy, can you spare a little change?" The raspy voice brought Liam from his drifting wonderland, and he was already formulating what kind of brush off he was going to give, something about having no money sounded good. *That's the worst thing about the subway, those damned panhandlers,* he thought.

As they slid into the stop, Liam looked at the beggar, taken aback. It was the man in the coat and hat. The one with the briefcase. Apparently, the lawyer had misjudged him. *He's a bum just like the rest of them.* The man, seeing that his question was not going to be answered immediately, pleaded his case, "I know what you're thinking, 'this guy's a bum,' but listen, I'm not. I can tell you're a working guy. So am I. I just…well this is so, embarrassing, but, someone stole my wallet earlier today, and, I mean, that's my credit cards, my cash, everything. I don't have anything that'd be of any value to you in my briefcase otherwise I'd give you something for a trade." The man tapped his briefcase and then placed it on the ground as if to illustrate his point. Liam knew where this was going and he was already feeling his ire beginning to rise. "Look, I only need five bucks to catch a cab, it's so late and this area isn't so good and…"

Suddenly, Liam was livid. He didn't know if it was the stress of the day finally catching up to him or just pent-up rage, but whatever it was, his adrenaline was pounding. *"Liar.* You're a damn liar. You didn't get your wallet stolen. You're nothing but a stupid panhandler who's too lazy to get a real job so you mooch off people who have one. Spare me your sob story. Life's full of them. You must think I'm a real sucker if you think I'm going to fall for that crap." Liam stared him dead on, then smiled menacingly. "Get lost."

Liam was shocked. He'd never really exploded like that before. Sure, he'd made outbursts in court, but those were calculated; this was unadulterated seething anger, and, Liam was surprised to find, he liked it. Unfortunately, the hostility was directed at a man who was a lot bigger than he was, and from the look in the man's eyes, Liam was certain he was going to get punched. But the attack never came, and just as fast as Liam had started the situation, the stranger ended it, flashing Liam a funny smile beneath the shadow of his fedora and, leaning a little close for comfort, saying enigmatically, "I wish you'd remember, *friend,* that to give your fellow man a hand or two when he deserves it is its own reward." Before Liam could articulate a response the man had already gone out the door.

Several moments later, the subway door safely closed, Liam had almost forgotten about the whole incident, thoughts of his troublesome case once again resurfacing. It wasn't until he heard frantic pounding on the door that Liam finally realized something was wrong. And it was not until he saw the very familiar trench-coated figure outside the window that he realized that something was very wrong.

Liam's heart lurched as simple rapping and knocking became full-fledged hammering blows, and the man in the coat looked strong. *He's trying to get back in,* Liam thought frantically, *he's coming back for me.*

Fear knotted into a tight ball in his stomach, and Liam was thankful for the thin partition isolating him from the obviously dangerous stranger. Liam didn't know what the psycho wanted, but vengeance came to mind as he desperately wished he hadn't been so snide with his comments.

The stranger punched the door, spidery tendrils weaving outward from where his fist had cracked the glass. Liam shuddered. No longer was this some simple panhandler asking for a few bucks, but a complete madman. Liam glanced around to see if any of his fellow passengers felt the panic he did, but he found himself alone, the subway car empty. *They must have gone out through the back door when I was talking to the psycho,* Liam thought frantically. What he wouldn't have given to be able to use that little fourteen year old girl for a shield. Even the one-legged guy could have provided some kind of diversion. But now, he was by himself.

He heard the man shout something, enraged. The crazy stranger screamed again, something about a case. *A case?* Liam's mind raced frantically. Was this something more than it appeared? A setup? He'd made many enemies over the years, all lawyers did, lost cases and lost causes. Maybe this guy was someone who was ticked about the way a legal case had turned out and was looking for revenge. The hat *had* been down, the lapels up, the face shielded from view. Wild thoughts and speculations flowed through Liam's head. And what was that about giving a hand to those in need? Liam swallowed hard. What if it was someone he had promised he would help and then let down? That happened all the time too...

Liam's line of thought was abruptly cut short as the man outside brutally threw himself bodily against the doors in an attempt to dislodge them. *Or maybe the guy is just plain nuts.* The lawyer shied away, retreating to the other side of the subway car, searching for anything he could use as a weapon, hating himself for never having taken any kind of self-defense class. *Crack.* Another violent blow nearly shattered the window, more seams in the glass spiraling away from the impact.

Only the sound of the train preparing to take off, melding with the muffled grunts and half-uttered curses from outside, broke the ominous echoing of Liam's heartbeat. "Next stop…" The words were lost upon him as he saw what was happening, the trench-coated man withdrawing a large fixed blade knife and inserting it between the doors. Liam's stomach heaved as he saw the stranger making progress at opening the door. The train started its departure, forcing the man to run alongside, hanging on to the knife.

Liam searched for some something to defend himself, anything, but found nothing nearby. The man's briefcase, alongside his own, sat on the other side of the car and, as much as he doubted either would prove much of a weapon, they could at least be used as a shield. But they were too close to the psycho. That was when Liam noticed the emergency brake cord. Weighing the disadvantage of the train lurching to a stop, with the possibility of help, Liam reached forward and yanked the cord.

As the train jolted to an abrupt stop, the man was still digging at the doors, trying to pry them far enough apart to get in. Just then a door did open, but it was at the far end of the cab, and Liam heard a voice, "What's the problem, sir?"

Time seemed to slow to a halt as Liam's mind made sense of what had happened. The voice belonged to a subway cop, a slight figure in uniform, but in the lawyer's eyes this new arrival was Hercules. Liam's words came out in a rush. "Oh, wow, thank you so much. I was so scared. There was this guy and he..." As Liam's eyes flickered to the door he'd been watching fearfully, he saw it empty and his words died off. The stranger was gone. Feeling very stupid, a grown man, worried over some *panhandler,* and now this little cop looking at him like he was some kind of baby, Liam chuckled instead. "No. Not really any trouble at all." The lawyer could barely breathe but somehow he found the constitution to concoct a plausible story. "This guy, this little punk kid pulled the wire. The door opened. You guys have got to keep a better watch on those hooligans. They're always disturbing my ride."

The officer looked at him quizzically for a minute, then merely shrugged, apologizing, "Sorry 'bout that pal. I'll keep that in mind." As the officer turned, he fixed the lawyer with a consternating look, as if what he really wanted to say was, *I'll be keeping an eye on you.*

Liam returned to his seat and retrieved his briefcase, suddenly everything falling into place. In reality it was kind of funny, now that he thought about it. In fact, the lawyer was almost hysterical busting up at his own foolishness, earning another disapproving glare from the officer. The whole thing seemed so stupid. Liam picked up the stranger's briefcase, which had been sitting on the subway floor the entire time, the reason for the whole encounter. That's what the stranger had been yelling for, his case. Not *a case,* but *his briefcase.* Liam felt a flush of shame, but it was a passing feeling. Maybe the guy hadn't been a bum after all. But he *had* left his briefcase behind, and to Liam the lawyer, that made it fair game. Finders keepers, and well, possession was nine-tenths of the law. It was the way the world worked.

Liam noticed the cop was staring at him as he tried the locks on his new acquisition, his problematic law case mostly forgotten now, this new treasure making the day seem almost worthwhile. "How come you have two briefcases?" the cop inquired.

Liam turned and answered with a dismissive air. He didn't like the officer. He was too smug, too in control. "Look, I'm a busy lawyer. That's what happens when you make lots of money, you've got lots of cases. But I guess you wouldn't really know about that, would you?"

Liam smiled a generously dry smile, and the cop made no further comment, now curiously studying the break in the window before finally just shrugging. Liam was busy thinking of how he'd jimmy the locks, when he gave it a try and found them unlocked. The case popped open.

Liam went wide-eyed. He couldn't believe it when he saw it. Filling the briefcase were body parts, dismembered human body parts, congealing in a sea of blood. Liam nearly vomited into his newfound prize, and he was horrified to see that most of the appendages were hands. His treasure was pool of human suffering, and then screams came unbidden.

It wasn't until the third time that he heard it. "Excuse me, *sir.*" Liam turned, his face aghast. A new kind of terror filled his eyes as he saw just what he was looking at. "I want you to remain very still and calm. Make no sudden movements." The officer had one hand holding his pistol trained on the lawyer and the other on his radio. Liam couldn't have moved if he had wanted too. "Yeah, 24-20, Request immediate back up, we've got a doozy."

Liam forced his voice to work. "But sir, you've got to understand, this case isn't mine." Fear crept into his voice with a faint sob.

"Sure, it isn't. Whatever you say, pal, it's not yours even though you just told me it was. Now don't move."

Liam looked out the window, his view distorted by the cracked glass, and swore he saw one dark trench coat after another, as he thought about his case and about the horror of possession. Liam could have almost laughed when he heard it, but instead he cried at the cop's unsolicited advice, "I'm telling you buddy, you'd better get yourself a good lawyer."

Summer's Day

Summer was burning the ashes, watching intently as every trace of her boyfriend's favorite blue shirt disappeared into the smoldering fire of burning leaves. She thought about just how much her boyfriend loved that shirt, and smiled a little, the engraved brass buttons the only thing she ever liked about it. She watched the tendrils of smoke as they wafted on the breeze, carrying away all the bitter memories of her former flame. She felt relieved, cathartic, as if now everything could be alright, as if this was the final symbol of letting go. She almost couldn't believe it was over, the years she'd lived in her ex's shadow. In the light of the hot autumn day when so many people were incinerating their piles of dead leaves, Summer reached up and touched the tender bruise around her eye, still wincing at the pain. It had taken unbelievable courage to finally get free, but Summer smiled, knowing that she was worth it.

As the fire subsided, she saw a glint amid the ash and shook her head, admonishing herself not to be so careless. Picking through the charred remains, she retrieved the engraved buttons of her ex's favorite shirt, and the bloodied teeth that had not succumbed to the fire, placing them in her pocket and preparing for the new day, knowing that he could never touch her again.

Give'em a Hand

The slowly congealing blood caking his hands oozed slightly as his fingers started to stir and the consciousness began to reenter his body. Nick's eyelids fluttered, his vision swimming as the first rays of light penetrated his pupils. The blurriness soon faded, but the splitting headache did not, the harsh incandescent light only intensifying his migraine. His head swam, his mind cloudy like a hangover after a long night of binging. *Had I been drinking?* he wondered, and then shook involuntarily when he realized that he didn't know the answer.

Where... where am I? Again it was a question for which he had no answer. Nick spoke aloud, hoping that somehow his voice would bring reality back into focus. "Hello? Anyone there?" There was no reply, and he found that even his voice seemed unfamiliar to his ears. Thinking back, his memory was dominated by a white outline, and a harsh voice, one tarnished by too many cigarettes. *Ironic.* The word struck a chord with him, seeming to come from the nether reaches of his mind, from the tiny crevices of his subconscious that still held some clue as to who he was. Nick shook his head, fear washing over him, feeling as if his memories were locked away just beyond his grasp.

Ironic. The thought came to his mind again, repeated in his head, as if his subconscious was desperately trying to tell him something. Nick almost screamed in frustration but then, slamming into him like a freight train, memories came. The white outline. The voice. The doctor. The cigarettes. That was what he had found ironic. He had commented about it before the surgery. "Here you are a portrait of health, doc, and you suck down two packs of those cancer sticks a day." That had been the day of the operation, the one that had changed his life, made him whole again.

As a wealth of emotions washed over him, Nick remembered more. He remembered the accident, the sharp sting of the saw's blade as it bit into his wrist, the sinew and tendons cut, the hand lying lifeless. He remembered the aftermath, the phantom pains, the feelings of inadequacy, of not being complete without his missing extremity. Finally, he remembered the joy he felt when he heard of the operation, the medical breakthrough that would allow for him to be whole once again.

The doctor had told him it would be a simple procedure, how advances in modern medicine made it possible to re-connect nerve endings and with proper anti-rejection medicine it would be possible for him to have the transplant. The problem, the doctor had told him, was finding a donor hand. Nick didn't have to wait as long as he had feared though, as the opportunity presented itself just a short time later. Michael Conners, a convict condemned to die and sitting on death row, had volunteered. No one knew the exact reason why, but Nick figured it had a lot to do with him trying to atone for his sins before his date with destiny came.

Nick wished Conners well and his good spirits were already starting to return after the strange awakening, when he noticed the blood. *Oh God no...* Not three feet from his bloodied hand a mutilated body lay in a crumpled a heap, vicious stab wounds marring the flesh. Noticing the uniform, Nick recoiled. *It's a cop... what have I done...* Forcing himself closer, hoping there was some other explanation, Nick realized that it was not an officer after all, but a prison guard. It was then that his memories returned in full. This morning he had decided to pay Connors a visit. What had driven him to he couldn't put his finger on, but he did recall his hand tingling, twitching ever so slightly, almost impatiently. He had gone through the motions, shaving, dressing, driving to the prison, but feeling empty as he did so, as if he were watching himself from afar. He remembered he'd had no conscious will to make a shiv and didn't even know where he'd learned to but he'd done it with precision, tucking it behind an over-sized belt buckle.

The prison officials had allowed him a private conference with Connors and he remembered the hideous ear-to-ear grin that split the convict's face as he was marched into the waiting room. But that was the last thing he remembered completely, the rest coming in fragments: Connors' assault on the guard; his hand tingling, withdrawing the hidden shiv; Connors seizing the weapon and repeatedly stabbing the guard; then blackness.

The memories returning, Nick felt ill and nearly vomited. Forcing himself to think, knowing he couldn't just lay there, he turned and looked at the body of the guard, as if in some way it might change before his eyes, that the guard might resurrect. The body sat motionless, though, and Nick noticed, with sickening clarity, that the guard's holster was empty. Almost on cue, he heard shots, six of them, three in quick succession followed by another trio. Then there was only silence.

The lack of sound, after the cacophony of noise seemed ominous, and Nick knew he had to move. He didn't get far, before the door at the far end of the room was flung open. "Hey, hey, Nicky, my boy! How'ya doin'? Come to visit your old buddy?" came an all-too-familiar voice. Connors stood in front of him, a large grin on his face. Then Nick noticed the gun in his lone hand. "Don't worry, I reloaded," he said a maniacal kind of glee on his face. "And I'm gonna get me outta here, that's what I'm gonna do. But there's one thing I need first. I need my hand back." He extended his stump to emphasize his point.

"I know what you're thinking, 'how the hell'd this happen?'", Conner chortled, seeming to revel in the moment. "Well, to be honest I don't frankly know myself. My uncle is a witchdoctor and he came and visited me and asked what I would give to get out of here. I told him my soul and he said if I was serious he knew a way. I thought it was a bunch of mumbo-jumbo to be honest but the candles and the chanting must have done something because here you are and here I am ready to go." Conner leaned close, and smiled. "I just need to reclaim what's mine."

Nick felt as if he couldn't move, frozen in place, each nerve ending unresponsive, each body part immobile, except one. Nick watched in horror as his own hand seemed to take on a life of its own, raising, reaching toward Conner's stump, almost as if missing its old home. "Amazing," Conner said, seeming equally astonished. "My uncle tol' me transplant organs can mess with the person gettin' 'em and his spell would take it a step further, but I never expected this." Conner paused for a moment. "You know, maybe I won't have to waste a bullet." He paused for a moment and seemed to concentrate. Then, suddenly, he threw his head back laughing and Nick could only watch in horror as his transplanted hand began moving toward his neck. Connors dropped the gun and pulled Nick's shiv from his pocket, chuckling wildly as he did. "Got to get it back quick after my ol' pal gets finished with you. Don't want no damage to my hand."

Nick's face contorted with pain, feeling the hand seizing him around the throat, sealing off his windpipe. Air came in short gasps and Nick struggled for even the faintest hint of oxygen. His lungs burning, Nick forced his unresponsive body into action, gripping the transplanted hand with his other extremity, trying to pry it away. Nick realized in horror that the exertion of trying to loosen the attacking hand's grip was only hastening the depletion of oxygen. The fingers bit deep, the pain excruciating as both sides of his neck were compressed under the pressure. Nick looked around through blurring tunnel vision, searching for anything that could save him.

Nick felt the strength in his good hand failing and he knew he didn't have long to live. He didn't know if it was a symptom of his oxygen-deprived mind or not, but a part of him wondered if this was what Conner felt each night on death row, the knowledge that his death was imminent. Praying that thought wouldn't be his last, Nick realized in horror that his right hand had dropped, no longer having the strength to fight. His vision narrowing to a speck, Nick saw hope out of the corner of his eye. Tapping into a strength he didn't know he possessed, Nick rolled toward the guard's body, forcing life into his obedient hand by sheer will alone. His fingers tumbled clumsily but in the end he managed to pop the button on the guard's belt and pull out the canister. Mustering one final ounce of resolve he pressed down on the button, seeing the red spray of cayenne pepper flying forth like the avenging sword of an angel. Conner sputtered and choked, grasping at his eyes and his mouth with his lone hand.

Instantly, Nick felt the pressure around his neck relent and he sucked in deep gasps of air. Forcing himself action, unwilling waste the opportunity, he grabbed for the gun with his closest hand. It was only after a moment that he realized he'd reached with Conner's former hand. Terror struck him as he envisioned the gun turning on him, but in the end it did no such thing, and Nick was able to keep his hand steady. "Not fun not being able to breathe," he said as he took aim, "but I'm sure it beats a bullet in the brain."

Squeezing the trigger, he was pleased to see his hand respond with no resistance and, in an instant, it was over. Conner was down and the nightmare was over. He felt as if the strange sensation that had plagued him since the transplant was gone. Lying back on the cool ground, hearing the sound of guards coming in the far off distance, obviously alerted by the gunshot, Nick closed his eyes. He could almost picture a civil award ceremony in his future for his heroism, and he almost laughed, envisioning a crowd giving him a round of applause, picturing everyone attendance giving him a hand.

A Stop Along the Way

A thick cloud of dust enveloped the Volvo as it raced down the desert road. The young insurance salesman driving checked his clock and cursed as realization set in. It was doubtful he could make it home by morning, even if he drove all night, and with how tired he felt, that wasn't a good option. *The last thing I need is to wake up in a ditch,* he told himself. As if it wasn't bad enough work kept him away from his wife most of the week, now this corporate trip was going to make him miss the day that they'd set aside just for spending time together. The meeting had kept him later than expected, and now that the stimulating jolt of several cups of coffee consumed over the course of the night was wearing off, he could already feel his eyelids beginning to sag.

Looking at his cell phone, the salesman cursed again. The battery had gone dead, the one that claimed to last six hours barely holding up for two, making it impossible to even call and say good night, or apologize.

Why didn't I just call her when I was leaving? He was bitter, but knew the reason why he hadn't. He had thought he could make it home in time. Making a mental note to pick up a bouquet of roses for the morning, he desperately hoped it would be enough.

Slamming his hand against the wheel, he thought of just how mad his wife was going to be. He could picture her now, setting the table with two plates, and probably candles to set the mood for a sensual celebration. She would be wearing that dress, the strapless one he thought she looked drop-dead gorgeous in. The driver shuddered and thought of the grim specter of divorce, or worse of coming home to an empty house with a note telling him goodbye. *She probably thinks that's what I'd do to her,* he thought sadly. *Doesn't she realize I'm doing this for her? Doesn't she know I just want her to be happy, give her the things she always wanted?* He shook his head, wishing he could just as easily shake off his uneasy feelings.

The salesman cranked up his radio, finding only static for one turn of the dial before stumbling upon a desert station, and mashed his foot down on the pedal, trying to quell his misgivings as he drove headlong into the night, listening intently to the radio program.

✳ ✳ ✳

A shimmering light in the distance caught his attention. As he approached, the tired man noticed that the glow, which at first he had assumed was a gas station, was in reality a small motel, nestled comfortably by the side of the road. He found something a little odd about its presence, seemingly in the middle of nowhere, but his weariness made the decision for him, the lure of a warm bed too enticing to give up. He threw on his blinker, and turned in for the night, stumbling from his car like a zombie, already half asleep. The old man running the night counter was studying a crumpled skin magazine with the same intensity a law student would study for the Bar.

"How you doin', Sonny?" the clerk said, not appearing particularly pleased to have to pry his eyes from his reading as he fixed the new arrival with a glare that implied, *why the hell are you bothering me, pal?* But the motel clerk said only, "Looks like you could use a cold drink and warm bed," in a harsh stereotypical western movie kind of voice, testament to a lifetime of hard cigarettes and even harder drink.

"You said it. That stretch of road is enough to put anyone to sleep. And a drink sounds mighty good right about now. Tomorrow's gonna be one helluva day."

The old man gave the new arrival an appraising look, his weathered features creasing so deeply, they looked as if they might stick. "So, you want a room, right?"

"Your best. Name's Gabriel Carter. I'll be paying cash and I'll need a phone."

"Well, we ain't got no rooms or no phones," the clerk said tersely, licking a dry finger and turning the page on his magazine. Just as Gabriel was about to say something undoubtedly rude, the old man smiled. "I'm just joshin' ya. We got a room open, but it ain't been cleaned yet. I'll get Johnny on it right now. But we really don't have no phones. No service this far out in the desert. Go'n get a drink while you're waitin'. I'll send someone when yer room's ready." He pointed the way with a gnarled claw of a hand, and added, "Who knows, pardner, play your cards right and maybe you'll get lucky tonight."

"Thanks," Gabriel said uneasily, not exactly knowing what the porno-perusing clerk meant by that last comment, but figuring his response was the safest one. *I hope he doesn't mean with him,* Gabriel thought, a sickening quality sinking in his gut, though he couldn't exactly place why. He chalked it up to stress and quickly headed off in the direction of the bar, wondering just how such an out-of-the-way place had almost full occupancy. *Maybe AAA gave this place five stars,* Gabriel thought sarcastically, as he watched in disgust as two small insects scuttled over something that looked unpleasantly juicy on the ground in front of him. *God, I hope that's not the kind of food they serve here.* But too tired to worry, Gabriel shrugged it off. He didn't care about anything anymore, except for getting a drink and going to bed.

The bar was virtually deserted, an old couple occupying a small table in the corner, sipping their martinis and reminiscing about days long since past, when politicians were honest and people respected their elders. It would have been cliché had the pair not been so affectionate with one another, every chance they got, giving a tender touch or a peck on the cheek. *Looks as if collecting Social Security hasn't slowed those two love birds down,* Gabriel thought with a slight tinge of envy. *Hopefully, Rachel and I'll still be doin' the horizontal shuffle when we're that old.*

The bar was black marble and had seen better days, the dried crust of spilled drinks overflowing from the cracks, and the bartender appearing in no hurry to clean it up. *Good to see he's doing his job,* Gabriel thought, then dismissed it. *Just as long as he pours a strong drink.* The man in question was old, ancient in fact, and bore such a close resemblance to the guy who'd checked Gabriel in, that for a minute he thought they might be twins. *Guess all old people do look alike,* he thought sardonically. The bartender casually leaned back against the liquor rack, a look of boredom clinched on his weathered features, as he said, "Pick yer poison, pardner," a more western movie line never spoken.

"Give me a double scotch on the rocks," Gabriel said as he slumped onto a bar stool. He downed it in one swallow. It burned like fire, but the pleasant afterglow made him order another round. This one went down even smoother, and the third smoother still. The bartender smiled at him, seemingly impressed with his new customer's appreciation of alcohol. Gabriel was already on his fourth round and feeling pretty good when his attention was drawn away from his drinking by a stunning young lady. She exuded sex as she entered the bar, auburn hair flowing lustrously over silky shoulders and a dress that looked two sizes too small in the bust, leaving little to the imagination.

In Gabriel's blurred perception the new arrival looked very familiar, too familiar. Struggling with his disbelieving eyes, Gabriel saw, much to his shock and confusion that the woman entering the bar was his wife. Somehow, someway, she was here. *But how?* It was impossible. He knew for a fact that his Rachel was at home, probably restlessly asleep in bed. The pleasant tide of intoxication made it hard for him to think, to make sense of everything, and at the same time soothing some of his misgivings, urging him to just go with the flow.

Never one to argue with good feelings, Gabriel ordered another round, for himself and the lady. *What was the harm?* he reasoned. The woman looked so much like Rachel, the narrow jaw line, the unflawed ivory skin, so familiar. There could be no other explanation. By the time she reached the bar, gingerly taking the stool next to him, Gabriel squinting and trying to bring her into sharper focus, he had made up his mind.

With a wide grin, Gabriel slurred to his companion, "Rachel?"

The woman stared intently at him for a moment, obviously puzzled before finally breaking into a coy smile. "Sorry, *hon,* but I think you're mixin' me up with someone else. Name's Crystal."

Hon? Now that was all wrong. And since when did his wife talk with a Texas accent? And use words like *hon?* No, that wasn't like Rachel at all. But if this was some new kind of role-playing game, like in the skin magazines, well, Gabriel was up for a little fun. "Well then 'Crystal', I guess you must've been in my mind all day, 'cuz I had you pegged as a Rachel." Gabriel didn't know if what he said made any sense at all, considering he'd just seen her about a minute ago, but right now he was too drunk, too excited, to care.

"Oh really," she said in that same cloying way that was overtly sexual. "Well, I guess in that case, hon, you can call me whatever you want."

Gabriel glanced down at his hand, and, seeing no wedding ring there, felt a tinge of alarm. A dim part of his mind wondered just where it had wandered off to, but another more dominant part was thankful for its departure, as he and his new lady friend tipped back their drinks. It just added to the game. Crystal took notice of his ringless fingers, and scooted a little closer, placing her hand on his leg.

"So, cowboy, how long are you plannin' on stayin' in this neck of the woods?" She was actually batting her lashes at him. Gabriel was sure he'd only seen that in the movies.

"For as long as you want, baby." Gabriel couldn't believe the words that were coming out of his mouth, and moreover, he couldn't believe that she was buying them. Not just buying them, but gobbling them up. For the next hour they talked and drank; five shots, turning into six, six into seven, and seven turning into an invitation up to the room. Crystal's response was typical of what Gabriel had seen all night, straight to business, all with that soothing croon, "Your room or mine?"

∗   ∗   ∗

It was the scent that woke Gabriel. Thick and musky, like trash left too long in the sun and his first thought was, *Great, I probably puked on her.* His eyes stayed closed, his head throbbing and aching like the ebb and flow of a tidal wave, a hangover in full force. *That's the last time I'm drinking,* among his first thoughts. Still waking from what seemed to be a dream, all too real and too pleasant to be true, involving a very sexy woman from the Lone Star state who could have been his wife but said that she wasn't, Gabriel raised his right hand with difficulty, finding his arm clinging tenuously to the sheets. He didn't even want to open his eyes. *Yup, I definitely yacked, and from the feel of it, this was a doozy.* He rubbed his temples and found them sticky as well. *What the hell?* With disgust, Gabriel opened his eyes and nearly vomited.

What he had at first taken as puke was, in reality, blood. Lots of it. Worse, as he turned, he saw, to his horror, that beside him on sheets that were once white lay the still, dead body of a woman. When Gabriel bent close to examine her, he saw, with growing terror, it *was* his wife. But how?! Rachel was at home, safe, probably enjoying a fried egg for breakfast. Yet inexplicably she was here as well, her throat slit ear to ear.

Gabriel's head didn't just ache, it throbbed, his heart beating at a jackhammer pace. *How could this have happened?* Panic threatened to overwhelm him as he looked around frantically. *Calm down. Think, dammit.*

The last thing Gabriel remembered was drinking. *The bar.* The bar downstairs. He had been enjoying himself, kicking a few back after an extra long day. He'd drank too much. Way too much. *It can't be her, Oh God please don't let it be her. It just can't be her.* Gabriel slapped himself, forcing himself to rethink the night through. *The girl. There was a girl. That's right, the one who kept playing games. What was her name?* Gabriel's mind reeled, searching for an answer. *Christina? Kristen? Crystal? Yes, that was it: Crystal.* He'd gone to bed with Crystal. A little thrill at an out of the way no-tell motel, but now there was this... whatever this was. "I didn't kill her!" He said it aloud and with such ferocity he didn't know who he was trying to convince. A horrible little voice in the back of his mind kept screaming, *"Murderer! You killed her in a drunken rage. Murderer!"*

A sickening tinge in his gut, Gabriel leaned over the body, examining it. There was no doubt about it, Gabriel thought, as he stared down at the corpse, coated in so much blood it looked like she had been born with red skin, images of modern artists who drenched their bodies in paint to create their masterpieces coming to mind. Still, despite the horror of the situation, a rivulet of relief surged through the fear in Gabriel's mind, as there was no question: it was Crystal. A deep-seated tremor had burrowed itself into the recesses of Gabriel's mind ever since he had seen the body, and no matter how inane it seemed, it was still there, the terror that he might have discovered a far more familiar face on the body. But it was Crystal, definitely Crystal. The girl who had so closely resembled Rachel in almost every way. The thought came unbidden, *even in bed.*

Gabriel broke down sobbing, his bloodstained hands covering his eyes. *What the hell is going on here?* He had very little time to ponder his predicament, or think of just what to do about it, as a knock at the door threw him further off balance. *What'll they think if they see this?* Gabriel felt the full onset of panic. He shuddered to imagine what someone would think if they walked in right now. *Think, Gabriel, think.* A bloody knife sat beside the body on the bed, the implement of the crime seeming to mock him.

The knock was repeated again, more vigorously this time. Gabriel wanted nothing more than to just curl up under the covers like he used to do as a child, and wish the bad dream would go away, until it finally did. "Go away!" Gabriel shouted vehemently but the knocking didn't stop. "Look, I'm busy! Leave me alone! Come back later." The handle rattled as someone outside tried to enter.

"Room Service," came the reply.

"Go away. I don't want any room service. Stay out!" Gabriel shouted emphatically. But the door lock rattled ominously. Seeing this astounding event unfolding before his eyes like a scene out of some horror story, Gabriel ran toward the door. "Leave me alone. For God's sake, just go away!" He felt pressure on the door, as the lock buckled and gave. Suddenly he was thrown back, landing on the ground with a painful thud, as the door was flung wide open. A scream came when he saw what lurked behind it. A minute ago he would have thought that the worst possible scenario would involve an astounded and upset housekeeper growing frantic while he tried to talk his way out of a hole, but nothing could have prepared him for what he saw.

The old man from the front desk stood hunched in the entryway, a look of pleasure etched on his weathered features. Gabriel opened his mouth, trying to form words, but none came. The clerk was getting closer now, and there was something terrible in his eyes, something *delighted*. His gaze swept immediately to the bed and the horrible scene there, actually licking his cracked and dry lips as he spoke. "Well, partner, looks as if you got *real* lucky last night, don't it?" Gabriel recoiled. "Now we can't just have all our clientele windin' up dead now can we? Gotta be doin' somethin' 'bout that. Settin' a right good example..."

Any response Gabriel might have mustered died in his throat as the old man withdrew a hand from behind his back, revealing a well-used ax, coated with dried blood. With murderous intent he hefted the blade, slamming it down at Gabriel. Luck and instinct saved him, barely, the disbelieving traveler rolling out of the way just as the blade smashed into the floor, the swing so powerful that the ax head became imbedded in the wood. *That could have been me,* a rational corner of Gabriel's mind screamed.

Gabriel backed up, still crawling, each scuttling movement seeming agonizingly slow. He hit the bed with his back, and scrambled up onto it, trying to put as much distance between himself and the obviously psychotic clerk as possible. As he fought with the bloody sheets, desperately looking for some kind way out of there, Gabriel jumped as he felt a hand grasp at his chest.

Gabriel screamed when he saw that the hand was Crystal's. There was only sadness in her eyes, deep wells filled with loss. *"Why, why did you let this happen...?"*

Gabriel, praying devoutly for this nightmare to end, searched around for something, anything, to defend himself. He pulled the reaching arms away, as Crystal continued to wail. Seeing a faint glint of steel, Gabriel lunged for it, and grasped hold of a knife, disgust filling him as he realized just what knife he held.

But instinct guided Gabriel and he didn't think twice as he sprang from the bed at the old man who was still trying to free his weapon. Gabriel wielded the blade at the clerk's exposed neck, slashing, feeling the sickening give as the knife sunk into the collar bone and beyond, driving the blade down to the hilt. The clerk sputtered and coughed, a thin hail of blood that looked like some kind of broken drinking fountain shooting into the air, soaking Gabriel's hand.

Gabriel didn't hesitate, using adrenaline-infused strength to work the clerk's imbedded ax free from the floor. He didn't know what was waiting between himself and his car, but he didn't feel like taking any chances. Soon finding himself in the hallway, he cursed. It looked so unfamiliar and was uncannily dark. He couldn't exactly remember how he'd gotten to the room last night, let alone what came after, so Gabriel had no clue about his location, but he felt confident. How big could an out-of-the-way motel be? Still, after everything unbelievable that had happened so far, Gabriel couldn't feel too sure about the situation. *One way's as good as another.*

Strangely, as he ran, Gabriel found himself immured in a sense of déjà vu, reminded of a time when he was twelve and had thought it so much fun to ditch his brother in a funhouse, constantly running through the dark, listening to his sibling's cries for help. An attendant had finally come to rescue his brother and Gabriel desperately wished someone, *anyone,* would step in and help him now.

He took a right around a corner only to find that the hall seemed to stretch impossibly into darkness. *What the...* His thoughts were cut off by a sound from behind, one that sounded very much like footsteps. Gabriel did the only thing he could do: he ran.

Gabriel's breath came hard as he stumbled into the shadows, the footfalls behind him coming closer. Gabriel couldn't bear the thought of checking over his shoulder, as the darkness that filled the hallway seemed to deepen and engulf him. Strangely the farther he ran, the farther he seemed from the end, and whatever was following was rapidly approaching.

A voice from behind caused Gabriel to scream, one from the impossibly long end of the hall. "Don't run, pardner! Ain't nowhere you can go. You gotta know that we're the law 'round here and you gotta pay the piper." It was unmistakably the clerk's voice. Gabriel cursed in desperation, stopping dead in his tracks. Running wasn't getting him anywhere. Impenetrable darkness surrounded him, casting him into a world of shadow. Then instantly it was pitch black.

Gabriel was out of ideas and out of time, with nowhere to go in this horrible indoor night. *Think.* His heart pounded, his pulse raced. As he hefted the ax over his shoulder, preparing to make a final valiant stand, a faint shimmer so small Gabriel had missed it at first glance, caught his eye. It was rectangular, the outline of light behind a door, penetrating the darkness. *It's still a hall. No matter how it's been twisted, it's still a hall.* Gabriel felt a slight sliver of hope. There was a chance.

In the complete blackness, Gabriel groped for a handle, fearing a clammy old hand grabbing him at any second, as he searched. Finally he grasped the knob, turning it desperately, only to find it locked. He drew the ax back and slammed it into where the door appeared to be, feeling it barely shudder under the force of the blow. *Why does it have to be so damn strong? What is this Fort Knox?* He could feel the hair on his neck rising as an inhuman cold seemed to permeate his skin. Gabriel slammed the ax again and this time the door gave a little, bits of wood exploding in a spray of chips and splinters. A gnarled hand clawed at him from the shadows as Gabriel swung one more time. The door shattered, splitting in half and Gabriel jumped through without hesitation.

Gabriel landed hard, but barely felt it, and instantly he was up and running. The scared traveler found he had somehow made his way back into the foyer, and that sliver of hope grew like an ember in a fireplace. He knew he could make it.

"Now you didn't think we'd let'cha go that easy, did ya pardner?" It was the bartender and he was blocking the door. The grim early light of morning glowed mockingly over the old man's shoulder. The man rested one hand on a tarnished revolver, a six-shooter, sitting loosely in its holster. Gabriel grunted, this time not in horror, but in anger. He'd come too far just to be thwarted now. The bartender's eyes positively gleamed. The old man was enjoying this. "Now what we have here, pardner, is a good old-fashioned showdown. You don't have yer gun so I guess that puts you at a disadvantage." He smiled, showing yellow teeth.

Gabriel didn't hesitate, even as the self-fashioned gunslinger continued on, *"Now what we're going to do is..."* He never finished as Gabriel's ax took him in side of the head with a sickening crunch. It happened so fast, without warning, that the bartender never had time to react. He was dead before he hit the ground. Gabriel had seen too many resurrections for one day, so he didn't stick around, fumbling desperately for his keys as he ran, praying he'd had the foresight to hold onto them last night. A moment of panic gripped him as he felt his front pocket and came up empty, but upon reaching his car, he found them buried deep in a back pocket.

Gabriel fired up the ignition. The engine thankfully turned over, a purring whir the sweetest sound Gabriel ever heard in his life. He threw the car into first gear and drove like a madman, never slowing, even after the motel had long since faded from the dim reflection of his rearview. He didn't stop until he made it home to the loving embrace of his wife, who had been worried sick. He'd had several hours to make up a plausible excuse to assuage his wife's anger and fear over why he hadn't come home. Not even sure himself exactly what had happened at that little out-of-the-way place, but knowing that even on the slim chance anyone would believe him, he didn't want to ever relive those terrible memories again. Instead he buried all thoughts of that little slice of hell in the far recesses of his mind, and never mentioned his experiences at the motel to anyone... ever.

Back at the motel, the being who had worn the skin of a clerk, now an androgynous flickering shape with no discernable semblance of form, communicated with another equally enigmatic figure. The pair would have been of great interest to UFO enthusiasts the world over, because it was obvious that the two were not of this Earth. They calmly discussed the matter of Gabriel, traveler on his way home, as if it were nothing more than a casual antidote, or a blurb in the morning news. "This one was by far the best, the most resourceful."

"Yes," replied the other.

"You do know I hate this."

A small portable television played an old black and white Western movie while the pair watched intensely.

"It's a dreadful necessity. Watch this now. The one called Duke will take both of them down." On the screen, the gruff, lovable, John Wayne shot and killed two of the roughest toughest outlaws west of the Mississippi. After the hoodlums lay dead in a dusty desert street, never to see the sunrise again, the conversation continued.

"Do you think the Council will be pleased with our results?"

"No. That human Gabriel in particular. If he is any indication of the rest of humanity, we may have a harder task ahead of us yet. On the television they seem utterly expendable, but in person..."

"It might be far more difficult than we have anticipated. Far more difficult..." Before his companion could respond, their conversation halted as they heard a car pull up outside. "Prepare your guise and get the room ready, we're about to have more company..."

*   *   *

The young insurance salesman snapped off the radio in his Volvo with a mild shudder, his heart beating just a little too fast. *I can't believe they actually play that scary stuff on the radio,* he thought as a cold shiver raced down his spine. He still couldn't believe that he'd found the "Haunting Radio Show" so eerie that he passed up a little diner in the old motel on Route 7, even though he was starving. He wasn't about to take any chances with old motels in out-of-the-way places. But Kyle, the salesman, had to admit one thing, the "Haunting Radio Show" had kept him entertained and awake on the drive home. *And that part about the wife...*

The bright lights of the city were already on the horizon as he continued on at his hurried pace. It seemed almost as if he had done the impossible, making it home in less than four hours. He'd never done it that fast or that exhausted before. *I still can't believe I made it.* Kyle said a little prayer of thanks under his breath, glancing up at the seemingly infinite sky littered with stars and wondered if aliens really did ever visit this planet. Then he pushed the notion aside, envisioning far more pleasant things here on Earth.

The Witching Chair

The chair frightened him. Jessie didn't know why, but there was something about the construction of it, the eerie way the polished rosewood seemed to resemble oozing blood, that put him on edge. The ancient strips of dried leather that bound the pieces of wood together looked like tendons and ligaments to Jessie, and brought to mind images of skeletons and other things long dead. Jessie attributed his misgivings to the over-active imagination of a fifteen-year-old boy, but still there was something unsettling about the chair. What made things worse was the way it seemed to have be purposely hidden away. He'd only stumbled upon it after testing—for what seemed like the hundredth time—a door that had remained locked ever since he'd come to live with his grandparents.

One glance had been enough, just peering into that room giving him the chills, and he knew he couldn't do anything about it, let alone ask his grandparents about it. Stern people, they would probably give him a whipping if they knew what he'd done. Still, the image of the chair remained in his head, tugging at his consciousness with each breath he took, like an obsession. The idea of that chair, and that room, invaded Jessie's every waking thought. He'd been close to asking his grandparents about it, any punishment seeming worth it to sate his unquenchable and interminable curiosity, but somehow, something kept him quiet.

It wasn't just that he didn't feel close enough to them to ask. Sure, they'd taken him in after his mother's death and his father's sudden disappearance, but there was something more, something about the strange way they sometimes looked at him that made him hold his tongue. In all his years growing up, before losing his parents, no one had even mentioned his grandparents. But now, they were only his caretakers, his only connection with the real world. Jessie couldn't help but remark on how he found himself in this strange house with its mysteries, immersed in a world of grief that was like a horrible nightmare he just couldn't wake from.

In a way, though, Jessie was almost thankful for finding the chair. It gave him something to keep his mind off the emptiness. Still, as the hours ticked by with painful slowness, and Jessie found that he could not pull his mind from that room, the curiosity began to gnaw at him like a bitter hunger. After three days of waiting, the questions lingering and festering in his mind, his hesitation and debating ceased. Waging war against an against an inner struggle, Jessie resolved that he had to get another look.

* * *

Jessie staggered back to his room after an unfulfilling breakfast, his head awash with thoughts. His grandmother, Constance, had told him that Earl was heading into town, meaning that he would be gone for at least an hour. Jessie didn't know why, but there was some part of him that told him that he shouldn't let his grandfather know that he'd found the room. With his grandfather's absence, that meant Jessie had a window of opportunity.

Moving to the old empty curio cobwebbed with dust, Jessie returned to the location where he had first found the room. Standing before the foreboding partition, Jessie couldn't help but think of how he'd reached the strange room in the first place. Jessie reflected on how he'd been exploring the house to kill the monotony and take his mind off of the pain of his parents' deaths. He recalled with a vivid clarity how his eye had caught on the faint outline of a doorframe, the wood carefully fitted to the point the crack was almost seamless. Jessie remembered his insatiable curiosity, how he had been attracted to the strange sight like a moth to a flame. He'd pushed and prodded, but the door hadn't opened. Even after Jessie had wrestled the curio aside, he recalled his frustration of being unable to get the impassive barrier to budge.

It had been like that the first four times he'd approached the strange door, on each occasion finding it locked. But he remarked on how the last time he'd come, the door had opened, and shown him the chair. Jessie thought back on his excitement, the sense of wonder mixed with fear he'd experienced, and found himself shaking a little bit as he stood now before the door, preparing to enter. Reaching out, he almost expected to find the way locked again, a timid part of him almost hoping for it, but instead he found the door creaked open easily as he pressed on it.

Jessie cautiously crept forward, glancing back at every step, expecting to see a leering face behind him, but he made it into the room without incident. The chamber was barren, as austere as he remembered from last time, a small attic alcove whose centerpiece was an old and weathered chair, no other ornamentation to draw the attention. A tremor of fear clawed its way into Jessie's gut as he noticed something he hadn't registered the last time he'd been here. The tallow-looking leather wrapping that kept the wood together wasn't just for binding the pieces into place.

Staring at two loose straps of yellowed hide hanging from the armrests and two straps that hung from the leg posts, a chill ran down Jessie's spine. His stomach knotted and he felt as if he might vomit, a part of him that he did not even want to acknowledge easily recognizing what they really were. *Restraints,* he thought, the very idea driving an icy spike of terror deep into his gut. Transfixed, Jessie stared at the chair, his soul recoiling in horror at the device and all its wicked implications. The horrendous chair terrified him a way he couldn't even consciously comprehend, his mind running rampant about all that it portended. His attention concentrated on the chair, he almost jumped in place when he heard the sound.

The faint echo that disturbed the chamber was almost a whisper, seeming far, far away, but Jessie couldn't help but admit that it seemed to be undeniably speaking to him. The words made his premonition all too clear: *"The truth, Jessie, you know the truth..."* Unable to handle the accusation, Jessie didn't wait around to answer, turning and running with all his might, not caring if he alerted everyone in the house, just wanting to get out. As

Jessie headed out of the room and down the stairs, back into world of sanity, he could hear the door slamming shut behind him, almost as if prodded by some invisible hand.

Jessie lay in bed, thinking of the incident. That was the only way he could articulate it, "the incident". His rational mind refused to accept what had happened, even though in his soul he knew what he had experienced. *A ghost, it had to be,* he told himself, though a part of him refused to believe it. Growing up in a strict parental household, he'd learned from a young age that the only thing real was what you saw in front of you. That's what dad always said, he reflected, but now he couldn't help but acknowledge how he had encountered something that just didn't make sense in his parents' rigid rational universe. *I know what I saw and felt,* he thought to himself, the revelation of that notion making him challenge all he had been brought up to believe. The troubling thoughts filling his mind, Jessie had feigned illness to his grandparents, spending the day in bed. But after night fell, and Jessie could not sleep, the thoughts dancing in his head, he had come to one conclusion: he had to go back.

As Jessie had pondered the strange idea more and more, he begun to get an intangible feeling that the plan was what he was *supposed* to be doing, that the room held the key to not just the mysteries of this house, but something deep inside himself as well. Jessie couldn't understand where he'd gotten the notion, but somehow, he knew he had to find out more. Jessie was resolute in his plan and after he was sure his grandparents had gone to bed for the night, he made the slow creeping journey back upstairs.

The top level was deserted, as Jessie knew it would be, but he was still terrified. Standing before the door, his heart pounded in his chest, his palms sweaty as he slowly made his way through the accumulated junk that blocked the entrance. White cloths draped many long-neglected items, but Jamie paid them no attention focusing on the door and bracing himself to enter. Pushing the door open, Jamie tentatively put one foot in front of the other.

Almost instantly after crossing the threshold, Jamie heard faint whispers. The sounds instilled him with a sense of panic that he could barely control but Jessie knew he had come too far to turn back. A strange intangible sensation told him that there was something here, something that he had to discover and Jessie pushed forward. Almost as if driven to do so, Jamie took one plodding step after another and rested his hand on the chair.

At first he felt nothing, only the cold rosewood, polished and smooth, but then his hand suddenly felt alight with fire, his blood seeming to boil in his veins. Jessie's vision blurred, his body feeling as if he'd plugged his fingers into an electrical socket. An intense agonizing shock flowed through every fiber of his being, the pain unique and almost impossible to describe, the injury feeling almost as if it was something spiritual, a stab at his very soul. A myriad of images, disconnected and disjointed, flooded over him, drowning Jessie in a sea of sensation, the visions appearing and receding like the tide in ultra quick motion. In the maelstrom of images, Jessie could make out scenes from his own life, images of his family, of happier times before his life was turned upside down. The searing pain intensified until it finally relented. Jessie unable to tell if it was a minute, an hour or even a day, but finally his hand came free.

Wearily Jessie turned, wanting desperately to call out for his father but knowing that there was no hope he would come. His shoulders slumped, tears welling in his eyes. His body wracked with sobs, and it was only after he allowed the cleansing tears to pour from his eyes that he was finally able to regain his composure. Wiping his face, Jessie looked up and realized that he was no longer alone.

"What did you see?" came a harsh voice, and Jessie nearly jumped in fear, seeing a figure that was all-too familiar and horribly frightening. His grandfather stood silhouetted in the door, but he looked somehow different, somehow *off.* Sallow sacks of flesh hung below eyes that looked as if sleep was a long forgotten friend and purple veins bulged in wrinkled skin of his sockets.

"Grandpa," Jessie said with a feigned comfort he didn't feel. For the life of him he couldn't think of anything else to say, his brain unable to respond. The only thoughts that were in his mind were of the strange circumstances of everything that had occurred in his life in the past two years. His mind circled back on memories of how his father had disappeared seemingly out of the blue, and how his estranged grandparents, who he'd never even met before, had come back into the picture. Now, staring at the relative who was almost a stranger, Jessie could help but notice how much his grandfather seemed to have aged since he'd last seen him. *Maybe it's the chair, Jessie reflected.* Taking a deep breath he tried to dismiss it as paranoia, but found it an impossible task, a part of his psyche reminding him how the door had been locked for so long and then suddenly it was open.

"Answer me Jessie," his grandfather said in a stern voice, one that sounded foreign and harsh, the sound like old gravel being thrown down a chute.

"I saw nothing," Jessie said, the nervous knot growing in his stomach with each passing second. "I just was admiring your chair. It looks nice." Jessie cringed as the old man in the doorway took a step, seeming to look even more haggard as he approached.

"Don't lie to me Jessie," his grandfather said, fixing him with a stern look.

Despite the tremor in his gut Jessie prayed for strength. Feeling a calm he did not know he possessed, he answered slowly, "No, that's it. Honestly."

There was a sly smile on the hunched man standing across from him. "You didn't touch it then?"

Jessie shook his head slowly. "No, I didn't."

"Liar!" the old man screamed, his voice a throaty growl. "You touched it and I know what you saw. You can't lie to me, not here not in this place of power. I felt the reverberation of the chair in my sleep. You should have never come here, not yet. I didn't think you'd find it yet, but now that you have there's little choice but going through with it."

Jessie wanted to scream but his voice seized in his throat. His mind awash with thoughts, Jessie barely registered his grandfather approaching. Shrinking back, he couldn't help but wonder if his grandfather had seen the visions he'd had of his family. *Had he felt what I felt when I touched the chair?* Jessie thought. Worse still, he wanted to know what the old man meant by "going through with it." The questions in rang in his head but there were no answers. A chill coursed though Jessie's body as he remembered the restraints on the chair. "I didn't see anything," Jessie said, his voice filled with horror. He didn't know what the old man had planned but Jessie had a feeling it was nothing good. Taking a backward step, his legs bumped into the chair. The feel of the wood on his legs was almost blisteringly hot. Just as he was about to bolt to one side, the old man was upon him, his gnarled hands grabbing and clinching down with a strength that belied their frail appearance.

Jessie squirmed as his grandfather wrestled him into the chair using what seemed to be an otherworldly strength. Try as he might, Jessie could not break away from the terrible hold. The old man bound his arms and then his legs with the restraints, talking as he cinched the clasps down tight. "It's time you know the truth, Jessie," the old man said with a grimace that looked horrid to behold, his teeth seeming preternaturally long and sharp. "I would've liked more time to prep you, the chair works better that way, but you just had to be oh so curious."

Jessie squirmed, trying to break free, all the while a part of him trying to register what his grandfather was talking about. Seeing the incomprehension in Jessie's eyes, the old man chuckled. "You really don't know, do you? Well, I guess it's time you learned the truth. You see, this chair's been in my family for generations, an heirloom of tremendous power. It's called the Witching Chair. I keep this room locked because no sacrifice should see it until the appointed time. But I must have been careless because you found it. Now you've given me no choice..."

"No choice to do what?" Jessie sputtered, panic engulfing him, thinking of the word 'sacrifice' and all it portended. There was no reply from the old man as he turned and walked to a small wooden cabinet in the back of the room. Jessie's heart beat furiously in his chest. Trying to get a response, any clue as to what was going on, Jessie asked, "If this chair's been in our family for generations, what's it do?"

At this the old man stopped in his task. His crooked back still turned, he began to laugh. "Not 'our' family Jessie. It's *my* family."

Confusion crashed down upon Jessie like a drowning tidal wave, and he could only sputter, "What… what are you talking about?"

Again came the horrendous laugh, "I'm not your grandfather. The old missus and I travel around and find people with marks of power, strong bloodlines, when our strength starts to wane and our age starts to show." Jessie tried to wrap his head around everything, but found himself unable to. "Like now," the old man said, turning. His face was a hideous leer, a monster's visage, a skull with flesh that seemed to drape from the bone. "In this room, you can see me for what I am, my age. But after you've given the chair your essence and your blood, I will be young again for a good long while. You see, boy, the wife and have been growing desperate. The strong blood isn't as easy to find as it used to be, and worse still it's harder with the advances of civilization to get the ones we need. It was easier in the old days." To Jessie's horror, he saw a sharp scalpel, one which seemed inordinately large, in the old man's hands.

"We had to set up a pretty elaborate deal to kill your father and get custody of you," he said, taking a step forward, "but from the fire I see in your eyes, and from what I know you saw when you touched the chair, I know it's going to be worth it. I only wish you could have waited a little longer, the sacrifice works better when you're on the cusp of adulthood. In any event, you're close enough. I have a feeling, with your fire, your blood is going to keep the missus and me young for a good long while."

Jessie's stomach knotted, the bile rising in his throat. His hand trembled as he fought valiantly against the restraints. The leather was too strong though, his flesh ripping as he tried to break free, and tears streaked down Jessie's face. The old man cackled again, "Feel free to squirm, those bindings are unbreakable. You're not going anywhere." The old man grew closer, his scalpel in hand. Jessie could see the rot of his teeth and the horrid jaundice of his skin.

"Please, let me go," Jessie said, pleading.

"I would never do that," the old man said, "you're the strongest we've had in quite some time, centuries even." The import of the words sunk in, and Jessie's head sunk, realizing that he was trapped, hopelessly ensnared. The tears flowed freely and did not stop. The old man mocked him. "Don't cry, boy, think of it as you're giving your short live to prolong my long life. You're like my retirement plan."

The old man who had pretended to be his grandfather reached out with his free hand, pressing hard on Jessie's forehead. Jessie's head impacted the back of the chair, the weight of the old man's uncannily strong grip keeping it in place. Jessie knew his neck was exposed, and out of the corner of his eye he could see the scalpel being brought up. Still, despite the fear, his contact with the chair seemed to be sparking something. Almost as if sinking into a dream, a strange sense of what could only be described as a foggy haze sinking over him, the colors of the world began to swim before his eyes. Absently, Jessie wondered if he'd already been cut, if his lifeblood was already draining and this was the beginning of death, the beginning of the transition to the other side. He could see the vague outline of a comforting figure coming into view beyond the old man and, in that instant, he realized that he was seeing his father. He saw something else too, the scalpel, still inches away from his throat.

Don't fight his grip, turn your head, a disembodied voice commanded in Jessie's consciousness, and in that moment he knew it was his father warning him. Doing as he was bidden, Jessie turned. The sudden change in pressure set the old man off balance, and as Jessie's captor tried to regain his grip, Jessie knew instantly what his father had been trying to accomplish. Almost as if in slow motion, he watched as the old man's hand, no longer having Jessie's forehead to lean on, slipped past and connected with the chair. At that moment everything went into lighting-fast motion.

The old man recoiled, as if he'd touched a live electrical wire or a rattlesnake, and Jessie saw his tormentor drop the scalpel in his lap and crumble to the floor, screaming as he did. The figure of his father began to fade, seeming to be doing something to the old man in the transition. The faux grandfather, revealed to be a succubus murderer, grasped at his own throat. Jessie registered a burbling gurgle, like the old man was being choked, and then finally his body lay still. Jessie exhaled deeply, sobbing, knowing the nightmare was over.

In a daze, Jessie fumbled for the scalpel and then he finally was able to get it in his hand. Jessie was midway through cutting the first restraint when the door burst open. "God please help me," he said as he saw the hideous abomination standing in the doorframe. On some level he recognized the mishappen and hunched form as the woman who had claimed to be his grandmother. However, any resemblance to anything anywhere near human stopped with the eyes, sallow flesh that seemed to hang like a wet blanket over crooked bones and grotesque veins engorged and protruding making the woman look like a monster. As horrific as the sight was, what was worse was the realization she was holding an ax in her twisted fingers.

"You killed Earl!" she screamed charging toward
Jessie. The monster hefted the ax high above her crow-like
skull, ready to deliver a killing blow. Her short squat legs,
though, gave her trouble running and Jessie mustered a
courage he didn't know he possessed and continued to
saw at the restraint. The woman beast was almost upon
him now, and as Jessie fumbled to cut the last remaining
threads of the restraint, he knew that there was no time
left. Still, something deep inside of him told him to press
on, a fire deep within his blood, and using the scalpel and
all his strength he wrenched his arm free.

The years of rejuvenation at the hands of evil
magic had taken their toll on the old woman and her
bones seemed barely able to hang together as Jessie rose
from the chair. Using that to his advantage, his youthful
reflexes making him just that much faster, Jessie threw
his weight to the side as the woman brought the ax down,
the blade of her weapon digging deep into the wood of
the chair. Jessie wasted no time, thrusting upward with
his free hand, the scalpel sinking into wrinkled flesh.
Blood that seemed more like red sand and dust than the
essence of life flowed over his hand. A choked gurgle was
all that escaped the woman's ancient lips as she fell to the
ground, as still and silent as a statue.

Jessie's heart beat furiously, and wanting nothing
more than to be free, he wasted no time in extricating

himself from the rest of the restraints. It was only when he was unfettered that Jessie began to relax. Staring down at the bodies of the monstrosities, Jessie knew there would be time to remove them later. Walking to the door, Jessie gave the room a long and sad look. After a moment, he turned and exited the room. Catching one final glimpse of the rosewood chair as he slowly shut the door behind him, he couldn't help but notice the ancient blood on his hand, and he couldn't help but feel just that much stronger, and that much younger.

Drained

Max was exhausted, completely utterly drained. It had been a demanding week, and the young lawyer felt every second of it. The intense crosses, the heated closing arguments, the nail-biting limbo of deliberations and then finally closure, the verdict. It had all taken its toll. *But in the end it was all worth it,* he reflected, sinking back into his ten-thousand dollar Italian leather couch. After all, it was cases like this that made it possible to afford his lifestyle. The city skyline stretched before him like a beautiful portrait, and Max poured himself another glass of Lafite Rothchild 1981 savoring the bitter dryness of the aged red liquid on his tongue. *I just can't believe the other guys are out partying,* he thought with amazement, *I just don't know how they do it.*

Almost on cue, Max heard the vibration of his phone. A quick glance at the screen told him it was his boss, a senior partner. *Probably wanting to congratulate me again,* he thought with a self-satisfied smile. "Yello," he said into the receiver.

"Max," came the voice on the other end of the line.

"Hey Peter, what's up?"

"You coming?"

Max shook his head, the smile not leaving his face. "I already told you at the courthouse, Pete, I can't. I'm beat."

"Hmmm… well that's a damn shame because I'm outside your apartment right now and you know how I hate being disappointed."

Max sat bolt upright. *Is this guy serious?* "But, sir, I mean it, I'm really really tired and I've already been drinking."

"So have I," came the reply. "Now get down here so we can paint this town."

Taking a gulp of the five-hundred dollar glass of wine, he thought, *so what, what do I have to lose? He's the boss, I can always call in sick.* "Okay, I'm on my way down."

✱ ✱ ✱

When Max saw the silver Aston Martin out front his heart lurched. *Boss or no boss, I don't want to be riding with Peter if he's drunk,* he thought, debating whether or not he should just go back upstairs. *Come on, you know that's not possible. You can't stand your boss up.* Still, a part of him wondered if it was worth his life. *Don't be silly,* he told himself, *if Peter was drunk he wouldn't be going out of the way to come pick me up, he's got better things to do than that.* It was well known around the office that Peter had a rolodex filled with girl's numbers that was almost as thick as the one with his client's. *He's not going to make it a mission to come and get me when he could be out with one of his supermodels,* Max thought, and found the notion reassuring, figuring that if his boss had made the trip he had a good reason. *Like possibly a promotion dinner...* Max smiled at the idea.

Walking over to the car, he was about to rap on the tinted window when it slid down suddenly. "Get in, Max. The night is young. You're going to the club."

Max was about to ask Peter a question, but he had no chance as the window rolled shut as quickly as it had opened. *What is going on with this guy?* he wondered, thinking, not for the first time that maybe his boss was on drugs. *It makes sense,* he reasoned with a lawyer's sense of logic. *There's no way Peter and all the rest of the firm could be out partying all night and still make it through their ten sometimes twelve hour days without the aid of some kind of amphetamines.* Max had remarked to his non-lawyer friends time and time again that there had to be something more going on, that there was no way that his attorney friends could burn the midnight oil like they did and still be productive. And yet somehow it was happening. *It's like they don't sleep,* he thought, going over the constant stream of wild tales he heard over the water cooler each day. *And now I'm going to join them…*

Gripping the handle to the expensive luxury sports car, Max prepared himself for a wild night.

✳   ✳   ✳

Three minutes into the ride, Max knew something was off. *Yeah, he's definitely on something,* Max thought, feeling the first unmistakable signs that this night could turn horribly wrong. Since they'd left the speedometer hadn't registered under eighty, and even though traffic was light, they weren't even on the freeway. *If he doesn't calm down, I'm going to end up on a slab…* Trying to take his mind off that unpleasant thought, Max turned to his boss, trying to ignore the fact that Peter seemed preternaturally pale and seemed to be sweating profusely, the strange pallor again making him wonder just what narcotic was flowing through his veins.

"Ugh, Peter," he started uncomfortably, "Can't you just tell me a little about where we're going?"

"No," Peter shot back sharply, his eyes glued to the road as the car rocketed around a taxicab. "I told you, it's a surprise."

Max slumped back miserably and it seemed as if Peter sensed his discomfort because he turned his gaze toward him. Max noticed, though, that Peter hadn't taken his foot so much as a fraction off the accelerator. "Look, you won a big case today. All you. I mean, sure we helped a little, but in the end it was only you and because of that you get the special lawyer club treatment."

"What club are we going to?" Max asked, thankful to be finally getting some answers.

"I've already said to much," his boss replied and an awkward silence hung between the two as they continued to drive through the night. After a minute Peter turned his attention away from the road as he dug beside the seat for something. Max was tempted to reach over and grab the wheel as the car didn't slow in the least, but in the end he sat motionless until Peter found what it was he was looking for. Pulling a small plastic water bottle from beneath the seat, Peter smiled. "Here you go, Max, why don't you sip on this to take the edge off?"

Max looked at the ruby-red bottle, not dissimilar from the vintage of bordeaux he'd been enjoying earlier. *What're we in college that we're pouring booze into water bottles?* he thought, but then figured that nothing about his boss would surprise him at this moment. *And what, he's pouring like hundred dollar red wine into a bottle?* Max shook his head, but said only, "What's the vintage?"

"Early millennium," Peter replied and Max was thankful that his eyes didn't leave the road.

"Wow, that must cost a bundle," he said before thinking, then, to cover up his faux pas, added, "to think you're putting it in a bottle."

Peter laughed. "It really doesn't ruin the vintage, despite what some snobs might think. Try it out for yourself."

Max took a small sip from the bottle, before nodding appreciatively. For being such an old vintage it had a remarkable sweetness. Then, taking another, larger, sip Max began to feel the heady rush of intoxication, savoring the mixture of salty and sweet. "This is fantastic," he said at last.

"Well, savor it Max, because where we're going, you're going to get a lot better than that."

*   *   *

There was no line outside and that made Max wonder. Peter, though, was reassuring. "That's the point of exclusivity," he said, "you don't have to wait around, jockeying to get in. You can only get in if you know it's there." Max saw the logic in that, and from seeing the interior, he knew he would have to agree. The opulence of his apartment looked like abject squalor compared to the club, though it was not at all what he'd expected. Ornate chandlers hung from vaulted ceilings and plush velvet couches sat in clusters around white marble tables. The ornate design that punctuated each and every detail of the décor stood in marked contrast to the dull and dingy dilapidation that marred the exterior. *We drive through skid alley in a hundred thousand dollar car and park in what looks like cracktown and then we come into this.* Max was thoroughly amazed. And the clientele was the best part.

Tinsel town studs and dolls didn't hold a candle to the crowd gathered in the club that seemed to have no name or identification whatsoever. The women wore corsets that punched up perky voluptuous breasts and the men wore silk shirts that shone chiseled physiques. *It's like a lingerie party circa Queen Victoria's time,* Max thought, finding himself aroused by a statuesque blonde who seemed to have not an ounce of fat on her toned frame, his eyes lingering on the curves of her buttocks, cupped in skimpy red lace.

Peter laughed, obviously seeing Max's lustful stare, and the young lawyer felt embarrassed. Almost as if he was reading Max's thoughts, Peter said, "Relax, Max, it's natural. I'm sure she feels the same way."

Looking down at his little pooch overlying former muscle gone to flab from long hours behind a desk, Max kind of doubted that. *It's like everyone here is a damn model,* he thought, not without a little jealousy. *So this is where Peter gets his harem. I've got to hit the gym more.* Walking behind Peter, he noticed, for the first time, just how toned his boss was.

When they got to the large circular sofa that was so big and round it resembled a booth, Peter took off his suit jacket and began unbuttoning his shirt, exposing his firm body beneath. Instantly, Max was taken aback and felt more than a little bit uncomfortable. Seeing Max's unease, Peter said, "Relax, this is a club unlike any you've ever seen. It's a place where a special group of people come to unwind."

Perturbed, but wanting to go with the flow, Max stripped off his own jacket, though he did not unbutton his shirt, feeling entirely self-conscious. "Well that a-boy," Peter said with a smile, "good to see you're loosening up a little." He said it with a tone that Max didn't quite like, making the young lawyer wonder just what his boss was expecting, that he strip naked and proceed to start an orgy. Shaking the notion off as nonsense, Max joined his boss on the booth-like sofa, craving a drink.

A waitress was quick in coming, and Peter did the ordering. "So honey, we're looking for two large glasses of vintage red, the darker the better."

Thoughts of a drink on his mind, Max tried to relax. Turning to survey the sea of beauty that seemed to surround him, Max again found himself astonished by the crowd. Many of the individuals were in the throes of passion, several vigorously making out while others were going farther, hands down each other pants. Max saw more than one exposed breast and in one corner it looked as if a group, two girls and two guys were all beginning to move beyond even heavy petting. *What the hell kind of place did Peter take me to?* Max wondered, thinking it might be some kind of strange sex club. *If he thinks I'm going to do something with him or in front of him he's sorely mistaken,* Max thought, his eye catching on a beautiful girl in a recessed booth, her top fully off as she locked lips with a statuesque man, a thin runnel of blood trailing down from his mouth as she forcefully kissed him.

These people are crazy, Max thought and he was about to get up when he heard a familiar voice. "Max! Buddy, good to see you're here." Max thought that sentiment was a hundred percent echoed as he saw two of his co-workers approach. It was Dan and Bob, both attorneys senior to him, but two great guys who Max knew loved to party. In fact, most of the crazy stories that he'd heard that hadn't come from Peter had come from these two. *And no wonder, they're cozy with the boss.* Max was about to breath a sigh of relief when the exhalation died in his chest. He noticed for the first time that Dan had his shirt completely unbuttoned and what looked like lipstick stained multiple parts of the collar. Still, that wasn't the most troubling thing. Bob's shirt was open as was his pants, his manhood hanging out unabashed. Any other time that would have troubled Max the greatest, but tonight that was the least of his concern. Two large gaping wounds just below the jawline drew Max's eye, the blood seeping out below.

Noticing the stare, Bob only laughed. "Well I guess I ruined the surprise," he said, a large smile never leaving ruby-red lips. "I'm sure Peter wanted to tell you, but seeing as I spoiled it, I might as well."

"What... what are you talking about?" Max was able to sputter. Prying his eyes away from Bob and his uncanny wound, Max found himself awake in a nightmare. All around him the carnal crowd of beauty was feasting upon itself. Pointed teeth tore into pale flesh, drawing blood, drinking as the sexual intoxication flowed though each being. Men drank of women and women of men, the liquor of life flowing into willing and eager mouths. "What…" Max managed through chattering teeth, "What is this?"

"This is your future," Peter said with a smile, "Eternity. A life without death."

"What do you mean?" he said quietly, trying to back away.

"I said you were going to the club and I meant it," Peter continued. "You're going to join the club. Every day you wonder how it is we're able to go out all night, to live the lives we want to live and yet still be able to work, to be successful. We can do what we want and remain beautiful. It's easy, really when you don't have to sleep." Max noticed, for the first time the fangs protruding from Peter's mouth. "The first step is the hardest, Max, but you'll thank me for it later. I'm initiating you into the world you've always dreamed of. I've been watching your performance and this last case cinched it, you're ready to be a member."

Max took another step, getting ready to bolt. The three lawyers were closest to the sofa and Max knew if he could continue circling then he might be able to get away. "I know what you are," he said at last, willing himself to be brave. "I don't want to want to live in a coffin and never see the daylight."

At that Peter frowned, "Come on Max, you're a talented attorney, I thought you'd at least be a little smarter and able to figure things out than that. You work with us every day. You have to realize that we can go out in the daylight." Max's head swam trying to think of what to say. "It's okay," Peter went on, "I know it's just the shock dulling your wits. It was the same with Bob at the beginning."

In that instant the waitress arrived with the drinks and Max knew it was time to go. Taking one step he realized his mistake. Bob was already behind him in an flash. "Too slow, Max," Bob said with a smile, baring ever so sharp teeth. "But super-speed is just one of the things you'll have to learn to deal with one you're turned. You see there are a lot of things about vampires that are really just myths." It took only a second for Bob's fangs to tear into Max's flesh draining life, giving eternity. As the blood washed over his lips, Bob laughed, waiting for the transformation to occur in Max. "But there is one thing that's true about attorneys, though, a lot of us are bloodsuckers."

Intersection

Paul's head swam, his eyes burning from the dust. Disorientated, he touched his head, his hands coming away sticky, as if coated in glue. When he saw the blood coating them, he screamed. Then he remembered. The bright lights. The Mack truck. Suddenly he glanced around, still aware of imminent danger, but found himself alone, lying on the ground without another soul in sight. Suddenly, a new fear knotted in Paul's stomach. *Why hasn't someone come to help me?* he wondered, shaking his head, trying to make sense of things. His muscles ached, screaming in protest as he tried to rise.

The town around him seemed deserted, a ghost town, and the absence of life was unsettling. *No one really knows what makes people quit a town, just up and leave,* Paul thought sullenly, reminiscing about all the towns he'd seen in his travels, places that just seemed abandoned. *But no one really wants to find out either.* To

Paul, it just reeked of something bad, something sinister. *What happened here?*

Blinking back dried blood from his eyelids, Paul surveyed his surroundings. Desolate would not even begin to describe it. *And the semi?* he thought. *Where is the hell is the semi?* He remembered the bright lights, and the crash. *The girl...* he thought, then stifled it. The Big Rig was gone now and he was alone. What he needed to find out was why.

Paul took in his surroundings, the dead town seeming like stereotypical Main Street USA. It could have been any small town in America, were it not for the dark windows and stores now fallen into disrepair. Still, something about it struck a chord deep in the recesses of his memory that he just couldn't shake. A traffic signal hung overhead, suspended from two intersecting wires, like the way they used to do it in the old days, the light faded out long ago. *How the hell did I wind up here?* Paul wondered. He would have sworn that he'd never set foot in this place before, but somehow it seemed oddly familiar. Shadows seemed to leer at him from windows, as darkened doors hung from their hinges in mute protest. The buildings seemed lifeless and Paul couldn't help but feel a pervading stab of unease.

A faint wisp flickered in the distance down the street, and Paul fixed on it. Looking closer, it appeared to be a woman, dressed in white, and she seemed to be searching for something, her hands outstretched and her eyes wide with fear. Paul averted his own eyes for a second, the vision seeming blindingly bright, and when he was finally able to turn his stare back, the woman was gone.

It felt like he'd seen a ghost. And the atmosphere seemed just right for it. *I must have hit my head a little too hard,* he thought and checked himself over with his hands, finding a few minor scrapes and some swelling in one of his legs. Other than that, Paul figured he'd fared quite well, considering. There was a nasty gash below his hairline, but the bleeding had stopped, leaving a mass of red ooze. *It could have been worse,* he thought, *much worse.* But somehow the optimistic idea didn't lift his spirits, the fact that he couldn't remember what had happened frightening him in a profound way. Paul lurched as he rose, trying to keep his balance. *Strained something. Probably the ankle.* Paul straightened up and took a tentative step. His ankle buckled, but held. *Strained, not broken.*

Paul tried to orientate himself before going on. His head still reeling, he took the time to tear some makeshift bandages from his shirt, wrapping his injured ankle for support in case he needed to run. Paul didn't like not knowing what was going on, the notion of trauma-related amnesia coming to mind, but he was always one who liked to be prepared. Ankle wrapped, Paul found a large piece of the metal on the ground, from what he assumed had been the accident. It would make a good weapon, a cudgel, and Paul once again felt the intangible frustration that he couldn't remember more about what had happened in the crash.

Hobbling, Paul started forward. The night seemed absolute, few stars lighting the skyline, their absence making the darkness more enveloping. It was almost as if the night air was palpable, coating the cilia in Paul's lungs, making his breath come short. He listened intently, trying to hear something, any sound that could lead him, but knowing deep down that he was really looking for the woman he'd seen. He felt a strange connection to her, a sense that they shared something, and that perhaps she might have some answers. He had no tangible reason to believe it, but inexpiably, at the gut level, it seemed to be right. As he listened, he was finally able to pick up something, a whisper calling softly for someone. *The woman in white?* he wondered, then chided himself, *Stop jumping at shadows. It's just your imagination.*

Suddenly, he found himself grateful for his makeshift weapon, feeling a sense of danger interceding. *The accident...* he thought and found himself wondering where the idea had come from. He couldn't remember any accident specifically, but he knew that there had to have been one.

Paul started walking, knowing he was getting nothing solved standing there, and it that was as good a solution as any. Waking up in this place in the middle of nowhere with no memory of how he'd gotten there had terrified him indescribably and he reasoned that the only way to make some sense of things was to get moving. Something else seemed to tug at his mind as he surveyed the seemingly abandoned town, the buildings appearing to shift ever so slightly as he watched. It wasn't ten paces later when he realized just what it was that had nagged him. *Laurel.*

This town is Laurel, he thought. *Not exactly, but close. God, how long has it been since I thought of that place? Five years? Ten?* He glanced about nervously, but there was nothing except for flecked paint on structures and weather-worn sidings.

Paul knew he had to find a phone. A phone call would help him make sense of it all. He'd call a cab. Did cabs pick up in the middle of nowhere? He didn't know, and for that matter, he wondered what would he tell them, *sorry pal but I really don't know the street address here, you'll just have to drive down a dirt road until you hit what looks like a dead town and then look for the crazy guy waving his arms in the middle of the street.* He stifled that line of thought. He needed to make a phone call to get back in touch with reality.

Peering into doorways as he passed, Paul searched for anything moving, any sign of life. His footsteps echoed in his ears. He glanced into a tailor's shop which sat situated next to an old-fashioned bait shop. Mannequins, like posed bodies, seemed to beckon with their static gestures, invitingly deceptive in their moth-eaten attire. A glimpse of something out of the corner of Paul's eye caused him to turn, hoping it was the woman and not something else. He was greeted only by a vacant street.

Trying to distract himself more than anything, Paul turned his attention to resuming his search for a phone booth. He already knew he wouldn't find one. Towns like this didn't have phone booths, and most of the businesses that even had phones were the rotary-dial type. That's why they still had the message about phones other than touch-tones on the operator line, because of towns like these. Another intersection led him to a street as desolate as the first.

"Where is this place?" he said aloud, his voice sounding awkward in the silent night. Deciding that one road was as good as the next, Paul turned the corner and realized one other odd thing. All along the street, and in the whole town, he'd witnessed a distinctive lack of technology, not just phones, but an absence of cars and street lights as well. In a hi-tech world where everyone seemed to be carrying a cell phone or a lap top, it was strangely suspicious. *How long ago did this town die?* he wondered, moving forward.

After a few more minutes of walking, Paul finally spotted a car, the first one he'd seen the whole time since awakening. Its appearance was made even stranger still by the fact it was sitting in the middle of an intersection. Paul, however, figured he still had to try his luck, heading in the vehicle's direction. What Paul saw as he approached made him recoil. He was still a distance away, but he could already tell something was off about the car, and his grip on the makeshift truncheon tightened. It was a late-seventies model, and Paul's growing trepidation turned to terror as he got close enough to glance in the window, seeing the crushed-in driver's side door and the thin filmy membrane of blood coating the clutch and steering wheel.

The windshield was cracked in places, soaked in a mass of blood and what looked like fragments of metal. Paul took a step backward. There was definitely something *wrong* with this town, and it was more than just this. It was everything. *This town looks like it gave up the will to live in the fifties and this car sticks out like a sore thumb,* he thought, remarking on the vehicle's strangely anachronistic presence.

Another backward step and Paul saw something in the car window. He scrambled away unaware that he was actually getting closer to the reflection he'd glimpsed. Suddenly, Paul's ankle gave, and he tumbled. The last sight he remembered as a cloud of blackness enveloped him, a sharp pain dully throbbing in the back of his head, was *a face, her face,* that of the ghostly woman in white. It was pretty, soothing, with flowing locks of blonde, but he could make out nothing more as his world faded away.

* * *

A faint lapping sound brought Paul from the darkness. His eyes seemed to bulge in a skull that seemed too small, and for the second time in a short period he found himself coming to with only faint pieces of what had happened sticking in his mind. Suddenly, as his memory returned to him, Paul turned his head, looking for *her,* and discovered the source of the lapping sound.

It was a dog, sitting obediently beside his head, tenderly licking the blood from his wound. The mutt's appearance was strange, but Paul was just grateful to find another living being. The woman was nowhere to be found, and for some strange reason, Paul had doubts about her existence. But at least there was the dog. Paul was already beginning to feel slightly better, knowing he was no longer alone. But as he stood up woozily grabbing his weapon from where he'd dropped it, he took a look at the animal and an overwhelming sense of dread filled him. Realization struck like a lightning bolt and Paul placed the dog instantly.

"Webster... Web?" The words fell from his mouth lifelessly, knowing that what he was seeing was impossible. Turning his back on the dog and all its implications, he hastened down the street, taking corners slowly at first then escalating to a full-on heedless run when he heard the dog's footfalls behind him, running almost playfully at his heels. Paul wanted to put as much space between himself and the dog as possible, cringing at the insanity of it all. It couldn't be Web, Paul knew, because he'd buried the dog ten years ago. Webster, nicknamed Web, had been Paul's dog, but he'd died, and yet he was trailing Paul just the same. Terror gripped him and he felt had to get out of there in a hurry, had to get away.

Paul took two corners quickly, afraid to look behind. A crash that sounded like thunder split the night air and made him jump, startling him to the point of faltering in his run. Paul swore it sounded like barking, and he dodged into a darkened alley, fearful of what may lurk there, but more afraid of having another encounter with Web, or whatever it was that looked like Web, following him. Paul dodged down one alley after another, wary of every discarded box and cracked window, each recess seeming a perfect hiding spot for an attacker. Paul's grip on his cudgel tightened. Panic pounded in his heart and he heard more loud barking, the noises seeming to get closer, fear fueling his steps.

Glancing behind as he fled into one alleyway, Paul crashed headlong into a chain link fence. Bouncing back, he cursed violently beneath his breath. Paul was careful not to put too much weight on his ankle, as he hopped the chest-high partition. Emerging from the alleyway, Paul couldn't believe his eyes. Sitting before him was the car. The same dead 70's-era car he'd encountered before.

Paul tried not to think about it as the barks seemed to get farther away, man's best friend losing the trail or giving up, and Paul wondered if he hadn't been a little too paranoid, letting the strangeness of his surroundings play on his imagination. *After all I've been through, I might have been over-reacting a little,* he thought, feeling a little better as he did, wondering if it really was Web at all or just some dog who looked enough like him to get Paul's already weary mind thrown into overdrive. Paul locked in on that line of thinking because it helped put his mind at ease somewhat.

With the cudgel still gripped tightly in hand, Paul started walking, trying a different road, ignoring the strange car and its bloody interior. He turned down Maple Street and smiled a little. *At least I don't see any dogs,* he thought, and blessed his mother for teaching him to be thankful for small favors.

Paul knew he still had to find a phone. Things were out of control and he had to find a lifeline back to sanity. He passed a broken window with a remaining painted portion proclaiming '…iller Brother's General', which seemed a promising place to begin the search. The inside was a cobweb-coated veneer of dust and neglect. Canned goods that seemed to have been around since old Ike was President were still standing strong on the shelves, displaying a proud layer of rust. *Fat chance of finding a working phone,* he thought, knowing he still had to try. A shudder coursed through his body, his grip tightening on his makeshift weapon as he saw two mannequins in the corner, a tarp partially obscuring them, tendrils of webbing providing a gossamer shroud over them. Paul's unease increased tenfold when he realized from the exposed portions that they were supposed to be hunters. Paul gave them a wide berth.

Walking around the counter, the store having the old-fashioned banister type of partition that separated the customers from the help, Paul found the cash register.

Just when he was about to give up his search and try somewhere else, he caught a glimpse of a phone resting on the other side of the till. Carefully, almost reverently lifting the receiver from the cradle, he placed it against his ear, praying for a live line. There was a dial tone and it was music to Paul's ears. A broad smile split his face, and he used the rotary, with what seemed to be agonizing slowness and clumsy ineptness, but finally he was able to dial the number for help. Time seemed to slow as he heard one ring and then another. He was too excited to realize something was wrong when someone picked up but there was no response.

"Hello?" Paul said, relief coursing through his veins. "Hello? Can you hear me?" There was no direct reply, but he could hear something, faint and far off, indistinguishable. Paul didn't care what it was, knowing that at least it was something. "Hello, listen my name Paul Hedges. I'm stuck. I don't know where I am or how I got here, but listen, there must have been an accident and..."

There was still no answer. It sounded like people were talking, like he was listening to a phone that was off the hook. Someone was prattling on about how they'd been so close. Someone else was very upset, asking what they could do. But it was far off, impossibly distant. He figured it had to be a crossed line. "HELLO!?" Paul screamed and then cursed, trying to hold back tears as he replaced the phone in the cradle. His hopes were so high. Picking up the receiver again, Paul dropped it when he realized the line was dead.

Spirits crushed, Paul sank away. He'd taken five steps when he heard the ringing. Glancing at the phone, knowing that things were getting stranger by the second, he shivered as he noticed that the phone wasn't even on the hook. Still, some faint hope drew him to answer, his steps heavy and hesitant, the ringing seeming terrifying loud. Receiver in hand, Paul cautiously put it to his ear. "Hello?" His voice was a harsh whisper.

"Paul." The voice was unmistakable with its drawl and it all rang home when he heard it, Paul's skin pocking with goose flesh. "Paul, is that you m'boy? So good t'hear yer voice. Now what is it yer doin' back in my shop after all these years. I mean, it's good ta have ya back an' all, son, after all this time. But yer needed elsewhere…" Paul knew the voice. It was a voice from Laurel. Old Man Miller, owner of Laurel's only General Store. That was what the sign on the broken front window had said, "Miller Brother's General Store". Paul's head was reeling.

"NO!" Paul didn't realize he was screaming. "No that's just not possible. This can't be happening. You're dead, Mr. Miller. I went to your funeral. You died when your car flipped on that road outside of town."

"Calm down, son, I'm just tryin' to help ya out from this side ta git home, we're all rooting for ya, and I gotta tell ya…" Paul slammed the receiver down cutting off the words, not knowing what was happening, just knowing that he had to get out of there, and fast. Those all too lifelike mannequins seemed to be stirring beneath their tarps, but Paul wasn't sure if it was just his imagination. Not wanting to find out, Paul quickly ran out of the store, feeling an overwhelming sense of *movement* as he did, as if he were being herded into something. The feeling was not pleasant. A quick glance back at the store showed only shadows.

Paul didn't care where he was going, only knowing that he had to get away. He made a quick dodge down one street and then another, each move he made seeming strangely as if it was going along some set path, as if he were being forced in some predetermined direction, no matter which way he turned. Four more blocks, each step more hurried than the last, and Paul found himself at his destination. It was the same car, but things were different this time. He didn't have long to register it all, things happening too fast, a sense of déjà vu striking him, only this time stronger than ever before.

As Paul approached the car, he stopped abruptly, feeling as if he had hit an invisible wall, his muscles freezing up. He saw the woman in white, beautiful as she ever was, sitting in the car with tears in her eyes. The car was dead, its battery had given its last final heave, bringing the car to the center of the intersection. The woman in white seemed to be in a panic, and Paul's heart ached to help her. Beside her in the car sat a little girl, barely more than a newborn.

They're in danger, Paul thought, instinctively knowing it was true. They both seemed panicked, and the beautiful woman was trying desperately to get her daughter free from her safety seat, refusing to leave without her. Suddenly, things became clear for Paul. What he was seeing was *the accident,* a memory coming into focus now and somehow transposed into reality. That was when he heard the sound of the semi truck, close now, so ominous and overwhelming that he didn't know how he could have missed it in the first place. Paul turned and he saw the semi that was the source of the noise, barreling down on the intersection, one tire shredded and lurching out of control. It was how it had been, Paul knew. The crash. The freak accident.

Panic gripped Paul as he watched the semi continue on a collision course with the trapped mother and daughter. An icy stab of terror sliced through Paul's ribs as he willed his unresponsive body into motion but it would not budge and he could only watch helplessly, trapped in a state of déjà vu, as the out-of-control Big Rig sped ever closer.

Paul willed his extremities into motion and in an instant he was at the car's door, throwing it open as the truck drew ever closer. The sickening sense of repeating the same action over and over again filled his head, everything seeming so familiar, so *wrong*, as if he had tried to save this woman and her child a million times and failed a million times.

The woman was still screaming as the truck leered closer. Paul pushed himself over her in a desperate attempt to free her daughter only to feel his bad ankle give with a sickening crunch as he went. Pain seared up his leg and the excruciating agony nearly drove him to collapse, knowing the same thing had happened countless times before and he had always succumbed. He could feel his world swimming away, and with it all hope of saving the woman and her daughter.

✻ ✻ ✻

"It's just not working," the woman said, with an obvious tremor of disappointment. "I felt like I was so close. Twice. The first time I could truly visualize me reaching out to him, and the second, well, I felt like I could touch him." She shook her head trying to keep the tears from coming. "I was so close and he was ripped away." She tried to look at the other people in the room, one man, another woman, her daughter and the doctor, but she found she couldn't meet their eyes. It was as if she had let them all down.

The doctor's white coat was dingy with wear, and he looked tired, but despite it all trying to keep a bright outlook. "Look, what we're attempting here is extremely experimental. You can't expect miracle results the first time we try it, Heather."

Heather glanced up at him, her eyes red-rimmed. "I know that, but it just, well, when you approached us with the idea it seemed so *right*, like it was a sign or something. I know we've all prayed separately, but I thought that we could reach him if we all were together, joining our energy."

The doctor would not be dissuaded. "I think it will work. This patient has been under my care for weeks now and he's fully healed, physically. It's mentally that he's damaged."

At this Heather started crying again. "And it's all my fault," she lamented.

The man who'd been praying with them, reached out his hand again, placing it on Heather's shoulder. "It's not your fault. It's no one's fault. My brother, Paul," he gestured to the patient lying still in the hospital bed, his body sound but his mind trapped in a coma, "was doing what anyone with a spark of humanity would do. He was trying to help you and your daughter. And he did."

But Heather didn't find it that easy to be persuaded. "Yeah, and how is he repaid. He's stuck in some kind of limbo and my daughter and I are fine."

At this, the doctor interrupted, impatient to try again. "Listen. Like I said before, Paul has been under my care for weeks now. His body is healed, but he can't come back to this world because he's trapped in his own mind, wrapped with guilt. I'm sure with the magnitude of the accident he's tormenting himself because he thinks that he was too late, that you and your daughter died in the crash. So what we've got to do is convince him of the truth, that you two escaped and it was *his* doing that enabled it. That, I think, is the only way he's going to be able to come out of his coma."

Heather burst into a new round of tears. "But that's what we've been trying to do and it's not working."

The doctor fixed her with a stern look. "That sounds like you're giving up. Did Paul Hedges give up on you when he saw a Mack truck barreling down on your stalled car? No. He ran to the rescue, freeing your daughter from her car seat. And we owe it to him to keep trying to reach him. I'm almost positive that Paul is trapped in a place of limbo, a place of memory, a loop if you will. I heard Paul repeatedly say 'Laurel.'"

"That's the town we grew up in," Paul's brother chimed in.

"Yeah," the doctor continued, "I checked it out after I heard him say that and found out it was where he was born. That's when I thought about the possibilities. In a lot of cases like these, where there is severe trauma, the mind reverts back to some place where it feels safe, like some childhood memory, only, judging from what I've heard Paul scream during the worst of things, I think his version of memory may be tainted because he feels guilty. The truck impacted right as Heather and her daughter got free, according to Heather's account, so Paul probably didn't even realize he'd saved their lives. He thought he was too late. Western medicine has never been too focused on the science of the mind, but Eastern medicine has been specializing in it for centuries, and when a case like this presents itself, where someone is healed, miraculously, in body and it's their mind that's damaged, it's time to turn to alternative treatment. So I read up on journals and I've been leading you through meditations to try to reach him. And now you're giving up before we've even truly started."

Heather tried to speak up, to deny it, but the doctor continued on, fire in his eyes. "We're going to try again right now, get our energy as focused as we can on reaching Paul, and we're going to bring him back." They all held hands again, believing. They sank back into their meditative state, the doctor leading them along the way as they tried, through sheer will to send their collective will toward Paul. There was no guarantee, nor even a good possibility that what they were attempting would work, but sometimes when it came down to it, all that was left was hope, and faith.

* * *

Paul felt a strange sensation, a tingling, almost like a direction of energy infusing him with strength and purpose. He felt as if he was being prodded onward, back into consciousness, and Paul seized on that imperceptible tremor of warmth. Suddenly, the world snapped back into focus and the sense of déjà vu left him instantly. This was uncharted territory. The woman in white, Heather, was yelling something, but Paul couldn't hear it over the sound of the thundering semi. Instinctively he knew what she was saying. Using his cudgel for leverage, Paul popped the stuck safety harness on the car seat and freed the woman's daughter. Heather grabbed the newborn and dove to safety, avoiding the out-of-control Mack truck's impact. The sound of the crash was deafening but through it all Paul could see something different, feel something different, a sense that the mother and daughter had survived, that everything was all right, and then there was nothing at all but light.

Paul's eyelids began flicker before finally opening, the light of the hospital room so bright. One hand came up to wipe away tears, as he was greeted, after all this time, by the sight of his brother. Heather and the doctor both had smiles on their faces. Realization set in instantly, and though Paul's voice was weak, his words were unmistakable. "Thank you."

Heather smiled through her tears. "No, thank you," she said, warmth filling everyone in the room.

About the Author

Eric Bonholtzer's work has appeared in numerous publications. He is a USC graduate with a Master's Degree in English from the California State Polytechnic University, Pomona.

Eric has received numerous awards for his writing including taking first place in the fiction and poetry categories of the College Language Association Creative Writing Contest as well as receiving the Ted Pugh Poetry Award. His short story collection, *The Skeleton's Closet*, is available at Amazon.com, Kindle, Bn.com, and other retailers. His poetry book, *Remnants & Shadows*, is also available. Eric's work has appeared in many anthologies and he is a regular contributor to several national magazines.

He is the author of the interactive text-based action/suspense game, *It's Killing Time*, where players are put in the shoes of a high-priced, world-traveling assassin. *It's Killing Time* is available as an iPhone and Android app, on Amazon Kindle, as well as personal laptop and desktop computer.

Visit www.choiceofgames.com for more information on *It's Killing Time* and visit www.ericbonholtzer.com for more of the work of Eric Bonholtzer.

In addition to writing, Eric is also a successful civil litigation trial attorney.